"Charlie will worry if I'm late…"

"Sure." Heath didn't know whether to shake her hand or give Ali a friendly hug. "Thanks for the assistance," he said instead. "You made this little bit a whole lot easier."

"No problem." Ali smiled. "If you ever want help, I'm happy to do it. I'm terrible at keeping my own house tidy, but I love cleaning other people's homes."

"Thanks. Tell Charlie hello for me."

"I will," Ali promised. "He won't be happy he didn't get to come, though. He likes looking through other people's things as much as I do."

Heath chuckled at her honesty as she let herself out the door. *Talk about opposites.*

She was just a friend, although he found her as attractive as any other woman who could pull his mind from his spreadsheets.

Too bad she already had a family—and a life with her bees.

Danielle Thorne is a Southern girl who treasures home and family. Besides books, she loves travel, history, cookies and naps. She's eternally thankful for the women she calls friends. Danielle is the author of over a dozen novels with elements of romance, adventure and faith. You'll often find her in the mountains or at the beach. She currently lives south of Atlanta with her sweetheart of thirty years and two cats.

Books by Danielle Thorne

Love Inspired

His Daughter's Prayer
A Promise for His Daughter
A Home for the Twins
The Doctor's Christmas Dilemma
The Beekeeper Next Door

Visit the Author Profile page at LoveInspired.com for more titles.

The Beekeeper Next Door

DANIELLE THORNE

LOVE INSPIRED
INSPIRATIONAL ROMANCE

LOVE INSPIRED®
INSPIRATIONAL ROMANCE

Recycling programs for this product may not exist in your area.

ISBN-13: 978-1-335-59892-9

The Beekeeper Next Door

Copyright © 2024 by Danielle Thorne

For questions and comments about the quality of this book, please contact us at CustomerService@Harlequin.com.

® is a trademark of Harlequin Enterprises ULC.

Love Inspired
22 Adelaide St. West, 41st Floor
Toronto, Ontario M5H 4E3, Canada
www.LoveInspired.com

Printed in Lithuania

MIX
Paper | Supporting responsible forestry
FSC® C021394

For your Father knoweth what things
ye have need of, before ye ask him.
—*Matthew* 6:8

For friends and family who have loved and lost.
Take courage, have faith and choose joy.

Chapter One

Ali Harding paid no mind to the barking dog in the distance when she walked out of the back door with a toolbox in one hand and a bottle of water in the other. The new beehives were still in their packages waiting to be assembled not far from the active colonies, and it was a warm, sunny day—the perfect time to work in west Georgia's unpredictable spring weather. The dog woofed again, and Ali squinted toward the Underwood property. Instead of an excited fur ball, she saw a man with wire cutters bent over her droopy chain-link fence. Ali dropped her things to the ground and watched. Mrs. Underwood had passed away last year and didn't have a dog.

Bees buzzed and wrens warbled in the fresh morning air. She watched the intruder pull up a section of fence while she tapped a thumb with her forefinger. He wasn't wearing a county service vest or any other identification. Ali's chest tightened, but she dismissed the anxiety when a black-and-white border collie burst from the trees and loped straight for him. The man dropped everything to wrap his tanned arms around the dog with a laugh. It was a scene that made her heart tug, but there was the fence. Her fence. And he was pulling it up.

With a groan at the thought of more to deal with on top of making it through a lean month, Ali strode past her garden and blueberry bushes. The border collie saw her and barked. The dog lover realized she was there and dropped the tool to his side.

"Hello?" She mustered a patient smile.

He stared for a long moment. "Hi."

Ali had only raked a comb through her hair that morning. She must have looked messy but wearing it down protected her from sunburn and stings. "Um, hi. I'm Ali Harding, and this is my land."

The man brushed his chest with an old glove. "Heath Underwood. I guess I'm your neighbor."

"I didn't know the property was sold."

Heath's smile flinched. "It didn't. My mother passed away six months ago, and I'm getting the place cleaned up."

"You must be Ms. Margo's son," said Ali as it came together.

"Yes. I have a brother who lives in New Orleans."

"I'm sorry about your mother," Ali assured

him. "I only met her a couple times after we moved here from Columbus, but she was very sweet."

"Thank you." The dog barked insistently. Heath picked up a stick and threw it, and the canine dashed away.

"He's yours, I presume?" said Ali.

Heath tracked the dog's course with brilliant blue eyes, and she didn't miss the faint smile of affection that creased the corners of his mouth. "Yes, Trooper's very friendly—don't mind him."

"I won't." Ali remembered the two hives she was supposed to be assembling and counted the hours left before she had to pick up her son, Charlie, from school. The day could get warmer, and time was short. "May I ask why you're cutting down the fence?"

Heath lifted the wire cutters as if it was a no-brainer. "The chain link's old, rusted and I don't want my dog to get tangled up in it again. He had a cut on his neck yesterday morning, and when I walked the property, I found this." He motioned at the fence. There were several small gaping holes with sharp edges.

Ali worked her jaw and reminded herself to practice patience. "That makes sense, but without it, I'll have more trouble with deer and other animals getting into my yard."

"It can't be that much of a deterrent," Heath

pointed out. "It wouldn't stop a squirrel or a rabbit."

"Yes, and I have my share of those." Ali brushed her bangs from her eyes but held her neighbor's sea-blue stare. "The problem is," she began calmly, "it's on my side, and I need to keep animals out of my hives as much as possible. Especially pets."

"Beehives?" Heath turned his attention to her backyard. "I thought I saw some strange boxes, but I hoped... Those are hives?" His tone pitched, but she couldn't tell if he was excited or horrified.

Ali tried not to beam. "Yes, I had twenty-four last year, just built two, and I'm building more this week." She looked back at her tools on the ground. "Next month I'll add the last set, so I'll have thirty producing honey by summer."

The man's eyes widened. "That's a lot of bees."

"It takes a village," Ali jested. He stared like he didn't understand. "To make honey," she explained. "Eventually, it'll be my primary source of income."

Heath's look of alarm merged with a frown. "How many do you plan to have in all?" Ali watched him study her land as if calculating the square footage.

"As many as I can handle. I have ten acres,

and we're surrounded by farmland, including your pastures, so there's plenty of room. I also grow blueberries and vegetables to sell at the farmers market."

"Thirty hives," repeated Heath as if she'd said she owned a zoo.

"Which is why I'd like to keep the fence," Ali reminded him.

Heath shook his head with a look of uncertainty. "The horses that used to be around here are gone. They sold them years ago."

"I assumed there was livestock once," said Ali. "I must have moved in afterward, because I never saw any."

"Those hives are awfully close to your home." Heath turned the subject back to her bees. "And mine."

"I'm sorry?" Ali wrinkled her forehead. The majority of her land was on either side of her farmhouse and the Underwoods' place, which backed up to hers, was a good quarter mile away.

"The beehives." Heath sounded oddly breathless.

"They're not unsafe," she assured him. "I wouldn't have bees if they were, because I have a son."

"I'm sorry, but I'm going to have to disagree about how safe they are, and I'm pretty sure the fence is on my side, by the way. My grandpa put it up to keep the horses in." Heath put his gloved hands on his hips like she'd said she dangled Charlie over the beehives whenever she felt like it. He had a trim waist that tapered down to long legs, and he was handsome in a quiet, almost rugged way with thick, dark blond curls he wore short.

Ali squared her shoulders. He was exasperating. "I bought this property three years ago, and I was under the impression the fence belonged to it."

"That's understandable," Heath allowed. "The farms around here are old and so are the fences. The city limits haven't reached this far out yet." He stopped as if contemplating a memory, then said with a sallow look, "I'm pretty sure you wouldn't be able to keep a million bees if it did."

"The bees are necessary for my business," Ali replied. "And just so you know, I'm licensed through the state. The sweet life is worth a little sting or two." She caught herself rubbing her fingertips together and looked down the line at what she thought had been her property. "It's legal. Limits aren't an issue. I assume you're going to put up another fence in its place?"

"What?" With eyes still laser-focused on her apiary, Heath slanted his head as if he hadn't heard her right.

"Will you replace the fence?" Ali repeated.

"I wasn't planning on it. I have a lot…" Heath glanced over his shoulder through the trees. "My brother and I received a letter from the county regarding the state of our property. There's a great deal of maintenance to do, and a fence isn't in my budget right now." When he saw her look of disappointment, Heath added, "I need to clear out some of these old trees back here this fall, too, and that's quite an expense."

"Is there anything you won't take down?" Ali blurted.

He hesitated in surprise. "I thought it'd be best to remove the weak or dead ones. Tornado damage is a nightmare to clean up, and we get plenty around here. It's good financial sense."

Ali ignored the fact he was right because she knew her bees loved the spring blooms on the flowering trees. "Speaking of tornadoes," she said impulsively. "I guess that means I'll need to put up a fence of my own."

Her neighbor gave her an uneasy smile, as if she'd called him out. "I'm sorry for the inconvenience," said Heath. He hesitated, then added with another frown, "but it's not like a fence will keep your bees off my side, either."

Heath Underwood wasn't sure if he should be unnerved or offended by his new neighbor, because he was overwhelmed by awful memories and the remnants of an adrenaline rush that had almost drowned him when he'd realized there were legions of bees behind Ali Harding's house. The diminutive fireball with woodsy-hazel eyes had gone from civil to boiling beneath the surface in a matter of minutes while he tried not to sprint away like she'd said she kept dragons in her backyard. He'd offered his hand for a shake when they parted, but she'd barely brushed his glove before striding off like he'd declared war. The problem was, he wasn't sure he could compromise. The rusty fence needed to come down to keep Trooper safe.

Besides, in his opinion, the real issue was her bees. He did not like them. Period. Exclamation point. Just the mention of them turned his knees to mush. It was worse than the mess his mother had left behind for him to deal with. Trooper at his heels, Heath hurried across the pasture he'd just hired someone to mow. He made a mental note to research the state requirements for beekeeping, although he suspected it was futile. This was Lagrasse, Georgia, and the rural areas had even fewer restrictions than towns when it came to livestock. With bee populations already in jeopardy, their rights would certainly supersede flashbacks of his childhood nightmare. That meant he was going to have a problem with Ali, because bees, in his opinion, were a menace despite their contributions to the natural world. The thought of so many stinging insects near his house made a shudder run down his spine.

Heath tossed the wire clippers into a rusted gardening shed that should have been demolished years ago and plodded over the ground to the carport of his ranch-style home, noticing the roof looked saggy here and there. He saw the sea of trash bags he'd left out had been picked up and sighed with relief. Wiping a smudge off his car with the hem of his T-shirt, he stepped back to admire the wax job, then tapped the key code on the side door to the house and let Trooper and himself inside. The smells of newsprint, dust and his mother's favorite lotion struck him in a rush of air, and the problems he'd momentarily forgotten sank back onto his shoulders.

"Ugh," Heath muttered then stopped to catch a sneeze. He sidestepped cardboard boxes filled with odds and ends of every description on the old shag carpeting. The sight of his father's bowling trophies made his heart free fall, but he shuffled to the refrigerator and swung open the door, determined not to wallow in self-pity. A package of Swiss cheese was aligned perfectly on top of the ham he'd bought at Piggly Wiggly, and he made himself a sandwich, eyeballing the progress he'd made cleaning the kitchen. The counters were empty, and the corners of the room were cleared of the shelving units that'd been stacked with knickknacks. He'd also removed all the duck and rooster lithographs, but there was still more clutter waiting. Pottery and cookware were piled on the top of the cabinets where dusty faux ivy dangled from the edges. Inside, decades' worth of dishes were waiting for attention.

After annihilating his lunch and musing over Ali and her fence protest, Heath plowed into the living room, reinvigorated. He patted his pockets for his glasses as he surveyed his mother's towers of books, magazines and newspapers. Across the room, family pictures mingled with seafaring paintings his parents had treasured. A large plastic tote of his father's models waited to be sorted on the hearth. Heath gave up on his glasses, plopped down beside the tote and pulled off the lid. He thumbed through bubble-wrapped airplanes and ships that his father had constructed with pride until his hand tremors had begun. The *USS Constitution* had been his favorite. Clay Underwood had taken his sons to Massachusetts to see "Old Ironsides" in person.

The doorbell rang and jerked Heath from his bittersweet reflections. His old high school math teacher, Monk Coles, had called him after learning he was in town and offered to buy one of the extra vacuum cleaners Heath had mentioned in exasperation. He waded to the front door and pulled it open. It wasn't Monk. The redheaded beekeeper gave him an apologetic smile. A wave of interest washed over Heath, but he told himself that it was because of her occupation, not the fiery hair and velvety eyes.

"Hi," said Ali. A small child of six or seven stood by her side.

"Hi!" repeated her mini-me.

"Um, hi?" parroted Heath.

"I don't mean to bother you, but I had a thought," Ali explained. She paused to look past him, and he pulled the door to his back so she couldn't see the disaster inside.

"You have a dog!" the child exclaimed as Trooper padded up to investigate who'd arrived.

"Yes, this is Trooper." Heath felt a smidgeon of pride.

Ali cocked her head. "Trooper? Are you a cop?"

For some reason, Heath wished he'd served in the navy like his father. "Accounting professor."

"Trooper? I think he's named after the *Star Wars* guys," said the boy.

"You would be correct." Heath loosened a smile, feeling an instant connection to him.

Ali motioned at her son. "This is Charlie. He's seven."

"Wow," said Heath, pretending to be impressed. "You seem pretty smart for just seven."

"I'm almost eight," Charlie lisped through a missing front tooth. "And I like dogs."

"Do you?"

"Yes, can I pet him?"

Heath widened the door, but instead of letting Trooper out, Charlie slipped inside and bounced all over him.

Ali sighed. "I'm sorry. We're still working on our manners."

"It's okay." Heath had no choice but to let her come into the house. It wasn't like she couldn't see the weeds outside. "Please don't mind the mess. I'm decluttering." He led her into the living room and moved a pile of blankets off the couch so she could sit down. Charlie found one of Trooper's balls and threw it down the hall. The dog barked with excitement and gave chase.

"So when did you move in?" asked Ali as Heath took a seat back on the hearth. She sat rigidly, hands gripped in her lap.

"About three weeks ago. I'm teaching online this semester because I knew there'd be things to take care of here."

"I thought I saw a different car in the carport last week."

"Yes, that's mine. My brother drove our mom's

car back to New Orleans. He needed it for his family."

"That was nice of you."

Heath shrugged. He watched Ali clasp and unclasp her hands while she looked around at all the junk. "My mother...collected," explained Heath. He made air quotes with his fingers on the last word.

"People do that," Ali replied. "I have a ridiculous amount of candles myself, not to mention antique furniture I plan to refinish someday."

Heath imagined the inside of Ali's home. Colorful, organized chaos, he'd guess, but she'd know where everything was stowed. "Mom wasn't too bad until my father passed away. Then the 'collecting' got worse, but it made her happy." Heath exhaled to hide his embarrassment. "I hired someone to come in once a week and dust when she got sick, but Mom didn't like people moving her stuff and insisted she didn't need help."

"She was just holding on to things she loved," said Ali. "I can understand that." She glanced down at a finger and twisted an invisible ring.

With a jolt, Heath suspected she was widowed. There was an air of loneliness about her if he looked past the confident and determined disposition. He cleared his throat, wondering if he'd deduced correctly. "It's been quite an undertaking, and I have a long way to go so I can get back to campus. She wanted one of us to settle down here, but I live in Auburn and teach at the university."

"You just have to choose what to toss and what to keep," said Ali, as if the bedlam was no big deal.

"I don't think she expected me to keep any of it," Heath replied. "She felt they had value and considered them investments. It was her way of leaving us something, I guess."

"What will you do with them?" Ali scanned the boxes of bric-a-brac around the room.

"I'll donate most of it, but I'll probably sell my father's models and extra household items when I have the time."

"That's a lot to deal with," Ali relented with sympathy in her tone. "What if you can't sell them?"

Heath floundered. What would he do? He couldn't throw them away. The thought of not passing on his mother's prized possessions riddled him with guilt. "I don't know."

"If you have any gardening tools you decide to get rid of, I might be interested," Ali informed him.

Heath raised his chin in agreement. "I'll let you know. We used to have a good-size vegetable patch, but I won't be keeping it up."

"Not your thing?"

"I don't have a green thumb," Heath confessed. *And I don't like bees.* "I don't enjoy landscaping, either, as you can see by the front yard, but I'm going to get it taken care of after I clean out the house. There's nothing worse than being the local eyesore."

"So you can't stand a mess, and you're scared of bees." Ali arched a reddish eyebrow.

Heath shifted uncomfortably at her observation. "How could you tell?"

She waved at the clutter on the floor. "Your boxes are sorted by category, and you turned as white as a sheet when I mentioned building new beehives."

"No, I'm not a fan of either."

She nodded. "Noted, which, by the way, is why I came over. I thought it'd be best to get the land surveyed. Just to make sure we know what our boundaries are…officially."

Heath processed her announcement, wondering if she still believed the fence was on her land. If she was right, he'd have to put a new one back up since he'd removed it. He'd also have to make sure it was a better one to keep Trooper from getting hurt. Suddenly, he saw the numbers in his balanced budget turn red, but fair was fair. "I suppose we could go in on the survey together," he suggested. Despite a possible storm that might take it out, a bigger, better fence might be a good idea after all, especially if she intended to put up more hives. Thirty bee colonies. The thought made his lungs shrivel. He took a measured breath.

"That would be nice of you," Ali relented, unaware of the anxiety she'd created. "To be honest, I don't have the extra money to put up a fence right now, but at least we'd know where we stand."

"Well, I don't intend to get any livestock," Heath informed her. "I plan to rent the house out for now." This seemed to mollify Ali, and the subtle awkward feeling between them dissipated somewhat. Her hair was the most beautiful shade of dark auburn he'd ever seen, but he brushed away the admiration and rose to his feet.

"I hope everything goes okay with your cleanup." Ali stood at the same time. "I'll do my best to keep the bees on my side."

Heath's heart tripped, even though he knew it was nothing more than a joke. "They swarm, you know, bees." He knew he sounded grim, but he couldn't help it.

"Yes, but I've never had a problem," Ali insisted. "I know when to split the hives." She narrowed her eyes. "Why do I get the feeling you've been stung before?"

"A few times," said Heath shortly. He didn't

want to go into details about how he was
swarmed by bees when he was a child, and he
certainly didn't want to talk about his failed
marriage, which still stung. He met her questioning eyes and arranged a stiff smile on his
lips, suddenly needing to be back in the safety
of his makeshift office staring at spreadsheets,
but Charlie and Trooper wandered in like best
friends, delaying his escape. The boy had his
hand on the dog's back until he saw the *USS
Constitution* on the top of the storage box.

"Wow, cool!" he cried.

He dashed over as Ali called, "Don't touch
anything, honeybee."

Heath held the ship up for him to examine.

"What is it?" The boy put his nose to the bow-
sprit. "Is that a pirate ship?"

"No, it's a battleship."

"It's awesome." Charlie leaned over to see
the rest of the contents in the box, and his eyes
flashed with awe. "I love ships. I'm going to
have a boat someday."

"Are you?" Heath smiled. "Do you want to
be a captain?"

"I think so," said Charlie thoughtfully. He
looked at his mother. "This year I'm going fishing for my birthday, aren't I, Mom?"

"Sure, yes," agreed Ali, her eyes darting to
Heath for a split second.

"That sounds like a fun birthday," Heath allowed.

"Yes, on the ocean. Do you like fishing?" The child looked like he was going to spontaneously combust with excitement.

Heath was impressed with his sense of adventure. "I like to fish at the lake. Do you get seasick?"

"Seasick?" Charlie laughed. "I can stay on a boat for days and days. Years."

"Come on, Charlie, we should go." Ali seemed anxious to leave. She turned back to Heath. "I'll let you know when I find someone to come out and do the survey."

"Great." Heath set his dad's ship back inside the box, noticing how Charlie's eyes followed his every move. When he straightened, Ali held out her hand, and he shook it, despite the odd feeling this wasn't business. Her skin was as soft as suede, and a wispy perfume—something rose—radiated from her. Heath met her gaze for a split second then jerked away and took Trooper by the collar.

Charlie raced for the front door. "See you later, Mister!"

"It's Mr. Underwood," Ali called sternly to the boy as she followed.

"Heath is fine," he shrugged. "Or Mister."

She didn't acknowledge his feeble attempt at

polite humor but gave a swift wave goodbye and shut the door behind her, leaving her alluring scent behind. Trooper yapped in frustration over his new friend's departure, but Heath let out a breath he hadn't realized he'd held. He sank back down onto the hearth and stared at a picture of his parents across the room. Ali was right. They needed to determine the property line if she was going to put a fence back up, although he didn't see the point. It might keep some creatures out of her hives, but it wouldn't keep the bees away from him until he returned to campus, and that was the real problem.

Chapter Two

Worried over the missing fence and puzzled about her neighbor, Ali took Charlie to Sunday school after a Saturday working in the garden, and they shared a potluck dinner with church friends after the service. Monk Coles made the mistake of telling Charlie his hound had puppies, so Charlie stayed at the retired schoolteacher's side talking his ear off about the new neighbor's dog. When Monk looked at Ali and said, "Border collie?" she nodded, suspecting he knew the Underwood family.

Then Sister Lovell, who wrote the monthly newsletter, piped up. "Is that house still falling apart? I offered to round up a cleanup crew and dumpster after Sister Underwood's funeral, but her boys wouldn't take me up on it."

"It's not in that bad a shape," said Ali. "The yard just needs work, and there are things to be cleaned inside." Others around her nodded with sympathy, but Ali saw knowing looks on their faces and cringed for Heath's sake. Then Charlie asked Monk if puppies drank milk, and to her relief, the Underwood property was forgotten.

By the time Ali dropped her son off at school Monday, she was grateful he'd forgotten about Monk's puppies, but he'd refocused on his upcoming birthday. It made her anxious with their honey stock low. February had been tight, and she'd barely made the payment on the business loan for the apiary in March. It was serious, because she'd used the house as collateral. All she had was room on a credit card for Charlie's fishing trip if she was able to make April's payment without a problem. After giving him a thumbs-up through the windshield, she headed downtown to see her cousin. Honey jars in the back of the car clinked against each another as she rounded a corner, calculating the income they might provide. Deep sea fishing was expensive. It was a big wish for a little boy, but his father had promised to take him on his eighth birthday, and she'd promised to keep it despite the fact they didn't live as close to the Gulf as they had in Columbus when Keith had passed.

Farther upstate, Lagrasse was just a tiny historical railroad town no more than six blocks wide. French immigrants from Savannah had built it among the Georgia pines that soared over the clay-packed earth of the region. Bushy azaleas lined the streets and bloomed in an assortment of purple, scarlet and salmon shades when daffodils peaked in the spring. Oak and sweet gum trees turned blazing colors in the fall. The main thoroughfare housed a police station and an assembly of small businesses providing flowers, antiques and clothing by consignment. At the center of town bubbled a rather Gothic water fountain, and down a slope that butted against the railroad tracks, the original small train station testified that Lagrasse hadn't changed much, but it'd endured.

Ali took Main Street to Loger hoping to survive the summer months. She pulled into a parking spot in front of the Gracious Earth. The natural foods store had a sign on the door flipped to Open. She inhaled mouthwatering fragrances from the Last Re-Torte Bakery across the street when she climbed out of the car and fetched the box of honey. Tiny bells over the front door sang merrily when she sailed through.

"Tam?" Her cousin and best friend was nowhere in sight. The store smelled like a blend of sandalwood and rose, quite different than the doughnut smells outside. She scanned the herbs and vitamins around the room as the distant murmur of Tamara Rochester's voice grew louder. The tall, light-complected woman with shining dark hair popped through a beaded curtain that camouflaged a door to the back. "Good morning!" Tam shoved a cell phone into the front pocket of her apron. "I thought I heard a guest."

"It's just me." Ali gave her a tiny wave.

"'Just me' is my favorite person next to Piper."

Ali grinned. "I don't mind playing second fiddle to your daughter. I'd worry if I didn't." Tam chuckled as Ali motioned at the honey jars. "I brought in more stock like you wanted, but the pints are getting pretty low."

"Good," said Tam. "I'm down to one jar, and Molly Grant asked where you lived last Friday since you've been out of the quart size for a while."

"Did she?" Ali wasn't sure if this was good or bad news. "I'm trying to make it go further since I barely met March's expenses."

"Don't worry." Tam hurried up behind the counter to peer into the box. "I don't give out your address."

"Good," said Ali. "I don't have the inventory for bulk right now, and I can't have customers coming to my front door."

"I know." Tam counted the jars by hand. "You don't need strangers coming and going with Charlie and the hives, but I still feel guilty making a killing off you."

Ali shrugged. "Don't. I owe you a lifetime's worth of babysitting and therapy."

Tam pulled a jar of Harding's Superior Honey

out of the box and turned it in her hands. The overhead light made the syrupy sweetener glow. "You know Piper and I don't mind keeping Charlie company." She glanced at Ali. "You and Keith were there for me. So have you set up the new hives?"

"Yes, a second pair. Two more to go."

"Do they have bees?"

"I ordered two ten-K packages yesterday."

"Wonderful." Tam typed something into her computer, and a sheet of barcodes began to print on the counter behind her. When the door chimes rang again, she waved at a bent man who toddled straight to the herbal supplements. She turned back to Ali. "I can't keep your stuff on the shelves now, so next year we'll set up a whole display."

"That'd be great." Ali could almost feel the stars in her eyes. "I should be finished testing lip balm soon."

Tam stopped in the middle of typing on her keyboard. "Have I said how proud I am of you?"

"Says the woman who quit real estate to open an herb shop."

"I'm still learning, but I'm earning," Tam declared.

"I'm getting there, too." Ali folded her arms over the counter. "I wish I made enough so I didn't have to worry about the loan payment every month, but I am proud of myself. I just need major growth this year so I can get through the winter. Thus the new hives."

"You're not losing money, though, right?" Tam yanked the barcodes from the printer and began sticking them to the backs of the honey jars. Ali shook her head, tossing around thoughts of the man who'd been on her mind all weekend. "No, but I have some extra things coming up. I still don't have enough saved for Charlie's birthday, and now I may have to build a fence."

Tam raised her brows. "What happened?"

"Do you remember that old chain-link fence out back? I know it wasn't doing that great of a job keeping critters out, but the Underwoods' son moved back to their house, and he pulled it up without even asking me."

"Underwood?" The lines in Tam's forehead deepened.

"Ms. Margo. The woman who lived behind me that passed away last year."

"That's right." Tam frowned. "The poor thing hung on for a long time, didn't she?"

"I don't know," admitted Ali. "She kept to herself."

"I saw the obituary," said Tam. "She didn't leave much behind."

"Just two sons as far as I know." The chimes announced another customer, and Ali lowered her tone. "The father died some years back, but I don't know from what."

"That's rough."

"I know," Ali whispered. "I don't know what I'd do without family while Charlie's growing up."

"So which son is it?" wondered Tam.

"The oldest, I think. He has the house, and he gave his brother a car."

"It's not much of a house."

"Yes, it's showing its age. He plans to clean it up and rent it out."

"That'll take some time. It's a mess," Tam observed. "Why'd he start with a fence?"

"To protect his dog from getting tangled in it." Ali frowned. "Can you believe he might clear out some trees back there, too? I'll never be able to keep that dog out of my backyard."

"I can see why you'd want a fence with the hives," Tam agreed.

"Yes, and then there's the liability," said Ali in exasperation. "He claims the fence is on his side, and he had a fit when I told him I had an apiary." She threw up her hands. "It makes no sense."

Tam's grin reached the corners of her eyes. "Tell him you'll give him some honey."

Ali pursed her lips. "He has something against bees, so he probably doesn't even like it."

"He's going to find himself in a sticky situation if his dog gets into your hives."

"That's another reason I came into town," admitted Ali. "I went by his house and told him I want to get the property surveyed. So I'm on my way to the courthouse to see if someone can recommend a company."

"How much is that going to cost?"

Ali wagged her head. "I have no idea, but I'm scared I'll have to use my credit card or ask for the extension I avoided last month."

The bells over the door jingled a third time, reminding Ali she needed to get out of her cousin's way. "Welcome," Tam called.

A pleasant voice said, "Thank you," and nearly gave Ali whiplash when she looked over her shoulder. Heath took two steps into the store and hesitated. Outside, Trooper gave a frustrated bark.

"Heath!" said Ali in surprise.

"You can bring the dog in," Tam called. Heath looked back and forth between them before walking back out to lead Trooper inside. The dog's tail whipped with excitement, and Ali held out a hand for him to smell. "Hello, handsome boy," she crooned, and Tam chuckled.

"What can I help you with today?" Tam asked Heath.

"I'm, uh…" He looked sheepish. "I was across

the street at the bakery and realized I've never been in here before."

Ali took in Heath's dark, fitted jeans and a periwinkle T-shirt that matched his eyes. He wore tortoiseshell glasses that made him look smart and attractive. Then there was the deep dimple in his chin she hadn't noticed before. "I was bringing my honey in," she blurted while commanding herself to stop the appraisal.

"We've been open for two years now," Tam said. "I supposed we're still a little new to out-of-towners."

"I'm from Lagrasse originally, but I live in Auburn."

Ali saw questions dancing in Tam's eyes. "This is Heath Underwood, who I was just telling you about." She gave Tam a hard stare, but the warning did no good.

"Nice to meet you, Heath." She pointed at herself. "Tamara. Or you can call me Tam like everyone else. I'm Ali's cousin, and live around the corner with my daughter, Piper. Welcome back to Lagrasse."

"Thanks. It's changed a little."

"Not much in the ten years I've been around," said Tam. "I hear you're a professor?"

He gave her a faint smile. "You heard right."

"Hmm," Tam returned. "So you're setting up shop here now."

"I work remotely." Heath glanced at Ali, but Tam wasn't finished. She held up a jar of honey.

"Have you tried Ali's honey?"

"Uh, no," he stammered. "I don't really..." He trailed off, and his cheeks turned a pinkish hue.

"You don't like honey," Ali guessed.

"Not really."

Tam laughed. "You were right, Ali."

"About what?" Heath inquired.

"Nothing," Tam assured him. "How long will you stay?"

"Through the summer." Trooper tried to wander, but Heath wrapped the leash around his wrist and pulled him closer.

"With your family?"

"No, just me." His gaze flitted to Ali again, and she wondered if he was pleading for help or annoyed she'd been discussing him.

"And Trooper," she offered.

He nodded. "And Trooper."

"You've inherited some beautiful land." Tam's tone was all flattery. "I understand you have big changes in mind. Already started with the fences?" Ali caught herself squeezing her eyes shut at Tam's insinuation.

"I'm just getting it cleared out. It's overgrown." Heath shot a look of suspicion at Ali, and she felt her face ignite with embarrassment. It couldn't be any more clear she'd complained about his fence demolition and disapproval of her hives.

"We have homemade pup treats if you'd like to check them out." Tam pointed across the store.

Heath looked relieved. "Thanks, I will." He gave Ali an accusing sideways glance. "And I'll pass on that honey."

She scooped up her empty cardboard box from the counter, telling herself she wasn't offended he didn't want to try her honey, but it felt as rude as taking down her fence. "I better go. I have a courthouse clerk to talk to about property lines," she announced.

"See you at the market on Saturday," said Tam. "Let me know when you get the new *bees*."

Ali did not miss Heath's jaw tightening at Tam's pot-stirring sendoff. "I will," she said in a flat tone. She gave Heath a small nod before marching out the door. "See you later, neighbor."

After his last online class on Wednesday, Heath called Monk, who'd left a message about the vacuum. They agreed to leave it in the carport in case they missed each other, and Monk invited Heath to come out to church before they hung up. He gave a noncommittal answer. He had no interest in running into old classmates or neighbors, much less communing with a God who'd led him to the wrong girl then taken his parents away. All he had was his career and a good dog. He wasn't angry, because they were enough, but he didn't see the point in devoting himself to worship when faith had let him down so many times before.

He changed into cargo pants and headed for the garden shed. He'd hardly been able to concentrate on recording his new lessons for his classes with all the other things he'd scheduled for the day. Not to mention, he couldn't stop thinking about running into town—and Ali—the other day. She hadn't seemed happy to see him again, although she'd been the one to come to his house to talk about a land survey. It didn't make sense to be so adamant about a fence when there was no livestock to worry about, and her annoyance over him cutting down a few trees was perplexing. Trees did not wander, he told himself, and they did not sting. Resolutely, he looked around for a can of spray paint and, finding nothing but green, tucked it under his arm with a pair of gloves and pruning shears.

Trooper bounded across the pasture behind the house as if he knew where they were going and needed to lead the way. Heath stopped to pick up the dog's favorite chewed Frisbee and threw it as far as he could. With Trooper diverted, he continued across the thick, clumpy grass, sad to see how wild it'd become. No longer used by horses or grown for hay, it was almost a hazard with animal burrows and thorny plants. Heath rolled up his sleeves as he approached the woods. Taking out his phone, he snapped a few panoramic shots of the tree line, then headed into the canopy that shielded ferns and trailing ivy he didn't dare touch. Several yards in, he stopped under a sprawling beech and looked into the branches. His old tree house was still there. Pleasant memories rose to the surface of his mind, although it looked like it was in worse condition than the house. The pitched roof was gone, and the railings had detached. The two-by-fours that had held up the platform looked questionable, and a few floorboards were missing.

Trooper barked, and Heath heard squirrels scramble up into the treetops around them. He rubbed the beech's spotted bark, struck by the realization that it had been around before his grandfather. He'd been a good family man like Heath's dad. And now Heath owned the land, but he had no one to share with it. No one to build tree houses for, anyway.

"What are you doing?"

Heath nearly jumped out of his skin. He whirled around to find Charlie watching him with Trooper at his side. "Hi, Charlie."

"Are you painting the tree?"

Heath chuckled. "No. I'm marking some that need to be cut down."

The boy looked up. "Is that your fort?"

"It was my tree house."

"I tried to climb up there last year, but I couldn't reach it." Charlie grunted. "Mom wouldn't let me have a ladder."

Heath noted the lower footholds were gone. "I can see why she wouldn't want you to bring one out here. That's pretty high."

"Can you help me get up there?"

"It's not safe," Heath replied in a sorrowful tone.

"Okay." Charlie's smile waned. "Are you going to cut it down?"

"I'm not cutting this tree down, but I don't know about the tree house."

"My dad would have built me a tree house." Charlie crouched to pat Trooper on the head. The dog had given up trying to herd him any further. "He died," Charlie added, matter-of-fact.

"I'm sorry," Heath murmured, flooding with empathy.

"Do you have a dad?"

"Not anymore." Heath squatted beside the boy and petted the dog with him. "He had something called Parkinson's disease and died eight years ago."

"What's that?" asked Charlie.

"It's a sickness that makes your muscles stiff." The boy's brows lowered. "He couldn't move?"

"He could move, but it made his body have problems," Heath explained. "He got sick with pneumonia and died. Pneumonia is like the flu."

"That's sad," said Charlie. "My dad was driving too fast, and he wasn't wearing a helmet." His voice cracked. "His motorcycle wrecked."

Heath smothered a quiet gasp. "What a terrible accident." Trooper tired of their attention and started toward the house, but then he stopped and looked back, inviting them to follow. Heath rose to his feet. "I know it's tough. I miss my dad, too."

"Yeah," said Charlie. "That's why I'm always careful." He looked up with a shadow of guilt in his eyes. "I mean, I try to be safe. I always wear my safety belt."

"That's good."

"But I want to do things."

"Like what?" Heath probed. They started through the woods after Trooper.

"I like to climb things and jump. I can do a flip on my friend's trampoline."

"There's nothing wrong with that."

"Sometimes Mom stresses out," Charlie explained. "I can't jump off the high dive at the pool unless she stands at the bottom and watches."

"The high dive? You *do* like to climb things."

"Yes," agreed Charlie. "I want to be a rock climber. I want to climb a mountain in the snow."

"I thought you wanted to captain a ship," said Heath.

"I want to do that, too," Charlie insisted. "Fishing would be a good job, and I could climb mountains on Saturdays."

Heath laughed. "I don't know about fishing, but I'd join you in the mountains. I like to climb, too."

"They have safety belts for that," Charlie informed him.

"I'll make sure to wear one," Heath assured him. "You're pretty adventurous."

"I like adventure," said Charlie. "It makes me like a superhero."

"Is that right?"

"Yeah. You can't have fun if you're scared all the time." They stopped and watched Trooper try to scramble up a tree. "What's he trying to do?"

Heath lifted a shoulder in a half shrug. "He's probably trying to catch a squirrel."

"Why?"

"He's a herding dog. His breed likes to boss around sheep."

"But you don't have any sheep," Charlie pointed out.

"I know," said Heath. "That's why I take him for walks and let him herd what he can find."

Charlie searched the tree branches for Trooper's innocent victims. "I only have bees. You can't herd bees."

Heath's chest tightened. "No, you can't herd bees."

The dog gave a whimper and sat beneath the old oak. "It'd be a shame to see that taken down," Heath admitted. "I think I'm going to keep it. The squirrels need a safe place to go when Trooper is on the prowl."

"That's a good idea," said Charlie. "How many trees are you going to cut down?"

"Just some of them," Heath allowed.

Charlie grinned, the gap in his teeth obvious. "I'll be able to see your house from my backyard if you cut a lot, but I'll have to go past the blueberry bushes."

"I like blueberries," said Heath. "I hope you keep them."

"We sell them at the farmers market," Charlie supplied.

Heath realized if he could see across the property once it was cleared, he'd be able to watch the beehives. At least he'd see them coming.

"My mom doesn't want you to cut anything down, but I think dead trees are okay," Charlie decided. "You should leave some for the squirrels." At the word *squirrel*, Trooper yipped and raced deeper into the woods.

Heath smiled at Charlie's thoughtfulness then remembered the tire swing his father had hung for him when he was little. "Come here a minute," he invited him. "I want to show you something." The child followed Heath with anticipation as he led him toward the house, explaining how he'd hire tree trimmers to clear the land in the fall. When they reached the pasture after discussing lumberjacks and pancakes, Heath pointed at a tire swing dangling from a tree whose limbs had grown out over the field.

"Wow, a tire!" cried Charlie in delight. He looked up. "That's a long rope."

"My daddy climbed a really tall ladder to hang that," Heath bragged. "I used to swing for hours."

"Do you still?" called Charlie, dashing for the tire.

"No." Chuckling, Heath followed him. Charlie scrambled onto the swing and began to spin in circles.

"Are you ready?"

"Ready!" Charlie cried.

Heath walked the tire back, then lifted it over his head and released it, watching the long, sweeping motion with satisfaction. Charlie hooted in delight as he sailed into the pasture then back into the woods again. "This is amazing, Mr. Heath," he shouted. When he returned, he waited until their heads were at the same level and cried into Heath's face, "Don't cut this one down!"

Heath laughed and gave the tire another push. When was the last time he'd felt such joy? He pushed Charlie for several more minutes, watching him change daring positions until Trooper bounded back from the woods. A quick glance told Heath something was wrong. The dog tripped and shook his head from side to side. Seeing Heath, he stumbled forward, but Heath jogged over to meet him halfway. The dog ran into his chest, whimpered and then dragged his nose across the grass.

"What's wrong with him?" Charlie called as the swing lost its momentum.

Heath shushed Trooper and ran his hands along the dog's back, feeling nothing suspect. He reached his snout, and Trooper yelped. "What is it, boy?" whispered Heath.

Charlie dashed up beside them. "Is he hurt?"

"It's okay," Heath murmured to Trooper. "It's going to be all right. Let me see." The dog finally lifted his head. There was an enormous lump between his eyes and nose, and his pupils were dilated with pain. A second bump was forming under his jaw.

"Oh, the poor boy," crooned Charlie.

Heath's heart picked up its pace as worry set

in. He didn't dare touch the obvious wounds, but he searched for blood. "You didn't get bit," he said to himself as he patted the rest of Trooper down.

Charlie leaned over Heath's shoulder. "It looks like he got stung."

Heath froze, and a closer look told him the child was correct. A fiery arrow of alarm shot through him, but he resisted the urge to jump to his feet and run for the house. When he looked around nervously, there weren't any bees in sight, but his heart still pounded like a sledge-hammer, and his legs trembled. Heath cradled Trooper against his shoulder with unsteady hands while his heart thundered with empathy. "Charlie," he said in a choked voice, "I need you to head on back home. Right now."

Chapter Three

Clenching the steering wheel of her little Toyota, Ali raced down the street and turned onto the two-lane highway so she could circle back to the Underwood property on the road behind her home. Thankfully, it was a straight shot to the vet's office in Lagrasse from there. She glanced at the tin of honey and herb salve she'd thrown onto the passenger seat after settling Charlie at the table to do homework until Tam arrived. Her cousin had promised to get there any minute when Ali called with the unfortunate news of what'd happened.

Her tires crunched on the gravel when she pulled into Heath's driveway, and Ali wasted no time jumping out after she turned off the ignition. She gave a thick row of yellow forsythia blossoms a glance of admiration as she rushed up the sidewalk. After she rapped on the door, Heath swung it open with a frantic look, and she heard Trooper whining from another room. "Charlie said Trooper got stung. Was it yellow jackets? Hornets? How many?" Ali noticed Heath's cheeks looked pale. "Is he okay?"

Heath left the door ajar and hurried away. "I think there're two spots. He's hurting, and he got sick in the grass before I brought him inside."

Ali dashed after Heath without waiting for an invitation. "Animals get stung all the time." She wondered if she should admit she'd heard Trooper barking not long before Charlie ran into the house to tell her what'd happened. The dog could have gotten stung in the woods, but it was likely that he'd been around the hives. "He'll be all right."

"Not like this," Heath said. She followed him into a tidy kitchen lined with burgundy-and-cream-striped wallpaper. The dog was on the floor in front of the sink. His face looked enormous, and he was drooling.

"Oh my gosh," Ali gasped. "He— I've never seen this before."

"I think he's allergic."

"I think you're right. Has he ever been stung?"

"When he was a puppy at a dog park once. We never went back."

Ali winced as she pulled out her phone. "That'll do it. Tam texted me the vet's phone number. Do you want to call? They're in town next door to Pizza Pies."

"I was just searching for offices on my phone."

Heath dropped to his knees and dabbed Trooper's snout with a wet cloth.

"Here," Ali said, fumbling with the tin in her free hand. "This salve may help. And let me text you the number."

Heath glanced up at her doubtfully but accepted the offering. After sharing the contact information, she crouched beside him and rubbed her hand along Trooper's back. "You're going to be fine," she whispered. Trooper let out a yelp of distress when Heath pressed a finger-scoop of the salve onto his nose.

"Let's go," Heath said in a low tone. "I don't want this to get any worse."

"I'll drive," Ali insisted. He didn't argue but followed her to the car, carrying the dog like an infant in one arm and dialing the vet with the other. After she buckled herself in, Ali backed out and hit the gas, torn between speeding and driving safely. "It's just five or six minutes away," she assured him when he got off the phone. They rode in silence just a breadth over the speed limit with the radio on her favorite country station. Ali scrambled to come up with polite conversation. "What do you like to listen to?"

"I like country and old rock," he said in a distracted voice.

"Charlie told me you have a swing?"

Heath mumbled, "Yes, I do," while staring straight ahead.

"He loved it," said Ali. "I haven't put one up. We go to the park. Seems easier." Heath rubbed Trooper's back with a taut expression. For now, the dog seemed to be distracted by the view out the window, but his snout still looked like he'd been hit by a golf ball.

"My father hung the swing when I was seven," Heath said after a strained pause. "Later, we built a tree house."

"Yes, I figured that was yours," said Ali, relieved he was distracted, too. "Charlie discovered it last year. He's always wandering off if I don't set firm boundaries."

Heath glanced at her. "He's just curious and adventurous."

"How about you? Are you adventurous?" Ali prompted.

"I guess I was when I was little, until..." Heath backpedaled as if he didn't want to share too much. "I like to do a lot of things, but it's been a while."

"You've been busy at the university."

"Yes. I like it there, although it's mostly students and families."

"Is that why you want to keep your parents' house?"

"Partly," admitted Heath, his gaze on the center of the road. "If I ever came back to Lagrasse for good, it'd be where I'd want to live. Maybe I will when I retire."

"It seems like a great place to raise a family," Ali offered generously. "I mean, if you ever wanted to do that." She realized she was digging a hole. Heath seemed to like being a bachelor, but he surprised her by saying, "I've been married. It was right after I earned my bachelor's degree, but we only stayed together two years."

Her heart filled with sympathy. Between his parents and a divorce, Heath had known a great deal of loss. "I'm sorry."

He flitted another look in her direction. "We just couldn't work things out after her dreams changed. I was still in school and needed time to accommodate her, but she didn't want to wait, so she set up house in Nevada and..." Ali heard him swallow. "Eventually she met someone else while we were living apart," he continued. "I bought Trooper as a puppy, and we got through it together." He gave the dog a squeeze. "I don't know what I would have done without him the first few months."

Ali gave an understanding nod. It wasn't her business, and she didn't want to pry. Especially since the man's dog had been stung, and he had a grudge against bees. "Dogs are great company," she agreed. They passed a few shotgun-style homes and then a bargain store. Finally, a sign with a chef spinning a pizza on it appeared. Pizza Pies. The vet was next door.

"I played Frisbee golf on a faculty team with Trooper," Heath divulged. "He's a great partner. Aren't you, boy?" He sounded shy, and Ali chuckled. The dog whimpered and rested his chin on Heath's shoulder.

"I'm so sorry he's hurting," said Ali. She took a deep breath to tackle the proverbial elephant in the room. "I hope it wasn't one of my bees." Heath raised his chin in acknowledgment, then fell into silence again. When she pulled into the vet's parking lot, he climbed out of the car before she could turn it off, and she had to hurry to catch up with him and pull the clinic's front door open. He murmured "Thank you" while still clutching the dog.

"I just called?" he said to a receptionist at a wide counter.

The young woman stood and inclined her head with curious pity. "Is this Trooper?"

When Heath nodded, the receptionist replied, "Poor boy. Not feeling well?" Trooper turned to face her, and her mouth dropped open. "Wow. You did get a bad sting. I'm Mikala. Let's get you in to Dr. Chahal and see what she can do for you."

Mikala hurried around a corner and opened

the door to the treatment rooms. Ali gave Heath a small wave as he carried Trooper back. She sat patiently in the waiting room, trying to relax by texting Tam brief updates. Tam informed her that she and Piper were at the house with Charlie making dinner. Ali sighed with relief. After scanning a few magazines for cat enthusiasts, she tossed one back onto the table beside her just as Heath came back through the door. He looked upbeat and calmer. "Is everything okay?"

"Yes," he responded, slipping down beside her. "They gave him a shot and something for pain. He's a little woozy right now, so she's going to give him a routine physical while we're here."

"That's a relief. Do they know what it was?" Ali's chest tightened, hoping it wasn't a bee.

"Bee stings," called the receptionist from the front desk.

Ali's heart flinched at the news. "You can tell?"

"A stinger was left behind."

"Oh," floundered Ali. "I didn't see it." She gave Heath a guilty smile, knowing that although it could have been any of a million bees, she did own that many. He exhaled, and it sounded like it was weighted with sadness.

The office door swung open again, and this time Dr. Diana Chahal emerged with Trooper on a lead. "We're all ready to go, family," said the cheery dark-haired doctor.

Heath jumped up, and Ali glanced at the receptionist, wondering if she'd been under the same impression that Heath and she were together. They weren't family, but there was no point in explaining it at the moment. "Feel better," Mikala called to Trooper. The dog looked sleepy but panted with contentment.

"You might want to keep him inside for a day or two," said Dr. Chahal, "and if possible, avoid going back to where he was stung."

"We were at home," said Heath grimly. He shook hands with the vet, and Ali led the way out of the door with a churning stomach. This was the worst possible scenario since meeting her quiet, serious neighbor. Charlie adored Heath, and she liked him also—despite the fence debacle—but a man with a dislike of bees would be hard to stay friendly with if his beloved companion got stung again.

After they settled back in the car, Ali turned up the radio to deflate a thin bubble of tension. She sang along quietly and was surprised when Heath joined her in a soft tone, knowing all the words. "I'm glad you're feeling better, Trooper," she called to the dog in the back seat. Heath had made him lie down on the floorboard. "And you're sitting down like a good boy."

"Can't be too careful," said Heath. "I forgot his harness."

"I'm glad you're protective of him," Ali replied. "Charlie may have mentioned his father passed away. He was in an accident. Keith was a big thrill seeker, and sometimes he could be reckless."

"Charlie mentioned he wasn't wearing a helmet," said Heath.

"Yes, while on a motorcycle." Ali paused to suppress a pain in her throat. The fading scar in her heart prickled. "It makes me a little overprotective when it comes to my son."

"I understand that," said Heath. He hesitated, then added, "But you keep bees, and you're getting more."

"Charlie is not allergic to bees."

"What if he were stung several times? Or what if it was someone else's child?" Heath looked over his shoulder at his dog.

"I would never put my son in danger," Ali insisted. "Bees are perfectly safe. A sting is an act of self-defense, so Trooper must have been around my hives if that's where he was stung."

"That's where most of the bees around here live, I presume," countered Heath. "You do know it's difficult for me to keep him off your property all the time."

"You could if there was a fence." Ali realized

her tone had a little more attitude than she'd intended.

"The fence had gaps in it and was as dangerous as your bees. Even Charlie could have cut himself. It was rusty." Heath's stare felt like lasers.

"Charlie is safe, and my bees are not dangerous," Ali repeated, keeping her eyes on the road. She realized they were on the precipice of a disagreement they might not be able to climb out of, and that would be unfortunate, since they were neighbors and all. Not to mention, she rather liked his blue eyes. "I mean, bees aren't dangerous unless you're allergic, which your dog clearly is. Are you?"

"Not that I know of," said Heath. "But if they were to swarm or to hurt someone, you could be liable."

"It's rare but possible. Having hives doesn't endanger anyone." Ali tried to maintain a reasonable tone. "Clearly, you've had an unfortunate experience."

"I was swarmed," Heath shot back. "They nearly killed me. I was in a medically induced coma for two days."

Ali felt her jaw sag. Her mouth went dry as she struggled for something to say. "When?" she stammered.

"I was eight," Heath replied, his tone lower.

"We were on vacation. I thought I heard flies around the back of a cabin we were renting and went out to investigate, but I got too close. They swarmed before I could get back inside, and I had close to two hundred stings." He gulped audibly as if remembering the terror.

"I can't imagine," Ali whispered, a ripple of sympathy shooting through her.

"I'm not comfortable around them now," explained Heath. "I don't wish them any harm, but..."

Heat and discomfort washed over Ali, and she cranked up the air conditioner as silence plunked between them. Heath didn't just dislike bees, he was terrified of them, and for good reason. When she pulled into his driveway, Trooper gave a happy bark. "I like your forsythia," she said, grappling for something positive.

"Thanks," Heath relented, and he gave her a sideways glance. "My mom loved having something that bloomed in the spring...to bring the bees to her garden." He smiled at the irony.

Ali gave a small giggle. "They do like them."

"She'd set out her seed pots on the front porch and watch them come and go."

Ali rolled her window down the rest of the way and rested her arm on the car door. "You must really miss her."

"I do." Heath climbed from the car and let

Trooper out. The dog trotted to the house. "Thanks for the ride."

"It was the least I could do." Ali clutched the steering wheel. "Heath?"

"Yes?"

"I arranged the appointment for a land surveyor to come out. If the fence was on your side, I'm going to put up another one when I can afford it."

He gave her a nod. "I guess it's something, although I hate to see you put your money into something that'll need maintenance even if it holds up in the windstorms."

"I won't have to worry about a limb taking it out if you're clearing the land." Ali sighed. "I hate to lose any trees on your side, but I guess there're plenty of other things to pollinate."

"Like your blueberries and garden," Heath reminded her.

"Yes, but they need so many acres per colony." She held his gaze. "I can't actually keep them on my property. You know that, right? They'll forage for up to a mile or more if they want." He gave a terse nod. "Don't worry," she assured him. "I know a local guy who handles swarms when they're looking for a new home. Like I said, it's rare."

"Right." Heath smiled, but it looked forced. "Thanks again for the help. Let me know when the surveyor comes out, and I'll meet you over there."

Ali waved. "Take care, then." He headed inside, leaving her alone. Heath didn't care about a new fence, she suspected, but he definitely wanted her to get rid of the bees. If she was wrong, and the old chain link had been his to remove if he wanted, her only option to do anything right away would be to use what she'd started saving for Charlie's birthday. It was a quandary. She couldn't let her son down, and she couldn't miss any payments on her loan.

It suddenly felt too quiet in the car, even with soft music on the radio. Ali remembered Charlie and Tam were waiting at the house and wondered if she should have invited Heath over for dinner. No. He wouldn't want to be anywhere near her place, and polite as he was, she didn't need anymore trouble.

Heath walked into the house with Trooper at his heels. The dog padded over to the couch as Heath carried the salve and medicine from the vet into the kitchen. He looked out the window over the kitchen sink, shoulders achy from bracing himself during the crisis and subsequent trip to the vet's office. Ali had been helpful, even though in the end, it had more than likely been her bees. It made him feel gnarled inside.

He was upset, but she wasn't to blame. He just couldn't understand why anyone would want to keep masses of bees around.

Trooper crept into the kitchen and went straight to the water bowl. "Are you ready to eat, boy?" Heath asked. The dog looked up with adoration and a noise of anticipation. It made the corners of Heath's lips stretch into a welcome smile. "I knew you were hungry. Me, too." Heath realized he could have invited Ali in, if only to offer her something to drink, but he needed to keep his distance from the beekeeper. His cheeks warmed with embarrassment when he recalled how he'd rambled on about his nightmarish accident. Being caught in the swarm had only lasted a few seconds, but the experience had scarred him for life.

He cringed. His former wife, Gretchen, deciding to move on after living apart for eight months had left a mark, too, and he hadn't meant to share that, either. He'd never been wary of women before, but Gretchen had ruined the perfect life he'd planned out. He'd become as circumspect around women as he was with bees.

But Ali seemed solid, he admitted. She had a cheerful maturity he admired, not to mention a funny way of making his breath snag in his lungs when she grinned. It creased the freckles on her face and made him want to rub his thumb across her cheeks to smooth them out. On the other hand, she was also headstrong, determined and only interested in making honey and raising her child. He snorted at himself for thinking about her and turned to the fridge to find something to heat up for dinner. They were just neighbors, and besides, he now had a fence problem and an injured dog to deal with because of the widowed single mother across the pasture who wanted to be queen bee.

Chapter Four

The doorbell rang just as Ali finished making several dozen honey sticks to offer as samples. She dashed to the sink to rinse off her hands and hurried to her front door. Tam raised a bag from the Last Re-Torte in the air, and Ali's mouth watered. She pushed the screen ajar. "Come in, please!"

Tam laughed, and they returned to the kitchen chatting about the darkening skies. "I need rain," Ali chirped. "It saves me the extra work and water on my watering bill."

"How's the garden doing?"

"The turnips are enormous, and the radishes and spring onions look great."

"That's awesome," said Tam. "I hope they go fast at the market this weekend."

"Me, too," agreed Ali. "I also have a few jars of relishes and pickles left to sell."

"Do you still have salsa?"

Ali winced. "Not many. I can't wait to see

what the new pepper garden puts out this year. I added another row of jalapeños."

"You'll be canning in your sleep," Tam teased. They dragged out bar chairs from around the kitchen island, and Tam dug into the bakery bag and handed Ali a chocolate-filled croissant.

"You are my very best friend in the world," Ali sighed.

Tam hooted. "I already was!"

Ali laughed and bit into the pastry with gusto. "I'm so glad I don't work within walking distance of a bakery."

"I tell myself I burn off the calories by walking there and back." Tam wiped her top lip with the back of her hand. "So how's Heath's dog? Have you heard anything?"

"No." Ali shook her head.

"I meant to ask you who paid for it."

"I tried to, Tam, but Heath wouldn't let me." Ali stared at the pastry in her hand. "But I'm grateful, actually."

"Hmm." Tam chewed her croissant.

"Hmm, what? That means you have a different opinion."

"I just meant that's interesting," explained Tam. "I wonder why he didn't let you pay for any of it."

"We don't know for certain that it was my bees," Ali pointed out.

"You said you heard Trooper outside around that time."

"True." Ali's shoulders sank. "I'm pretty sure that's when it happened."

"You should have insisted on covering it," said Tam.

"Why?"

"Liability. You do have insurance for that sort of thing, don't you?"

"I'm not sure if that covers a dog." Ali brushed a few stray crumbs off her lap. "I was so worried about Heath being upset and stressing about my finances I didn't insist."

Tam let out a quiet breath. "I can't imagine being swarmed. It must have been awful."

"Me, either," agreed Ali. "He didn't say if it was honeybees."

"Regardless, I'd recommend offering him something," suggested Tam. "Remember when I got sued for not informing a customer of the ingredients in my loose teas?"

"You won that case." Ali frowned.

"Yes, because they were labeled on the dispensers," Tam reminded her. "I'm more careful now. I have laminated cards reminding everyone to check the products for their own allergens."

"Who's allergic to oranges, anyway?" grumbled Ali.

"You'd be surprised." Tam crumpled the bakery bag in her hands. "Uncle Brian is allergic to watermelon, remember? Is Heath allergic to bees after all that?"

"I don't think so, but we know Trooper is." Ali's chest constricted despite the delicious remnants of chocolate in her mouth. Tam was right. She should have offered to pay Trooper's vet bill just to cover her bases, even though the dog had probably been on her property. She scowled. "If Heath had left that fence up, Trooper wouldn't have wandered over."

"Dogs." Tam shrugged. "You never know. He could have jumped over it if he wanted to anyway, and it was pretty old."

"Yes, but at least it was an obvious boundary. I'll drop by the Underwoods' after I pick up Charlie from school and offer again."

"Or you could before." Tam winked at her.

Ali's cheeks warmed. "Why? Charlie likes him."

"Yes, but Charlie's always around."

"So?"

"I saw how you two behaved when Heath came into the shop."

"We were practically arguing," said Ali.

"No, you weren't. You had a very intense conversation and couldn't keep your eyes off each other for the whole of it."

Ali forced a laugh. "That's not true."

Tam raised her eyebrows. "He seems nice and smart, and you can't ignore those blue peepers."

"They only look that blue because of his complexion."

"How does an accounting professor get so tan?"

"He walks his dog and takes down fences," retorted Ali.

"So he likes the outdoors—relatively." Tam began to tick off facts on her fingers. "He loved his parents. He has a career. He's willing to discuss and work out differences, and Charlie likes him, plus he babies his dog." She grinned slyly at Ali. "Not to mention, he's easy on the eyes."

Ali swatted at her playfully. "Stop it. He's already been married, and he's grieving. So am I, so I can relate."

"You've come a long way," Tam observed.

"I am in a better place, finances notwithstanding," agreed Ali.

"So?" Tam pressed.

"So what?"

"What's stopping you from considering something new with someone besides your son and your bees?"

Ali hopped out of her chair and hurried over to put her napkin in the trash. Outside the window, a midday shower sprinkled rain against the siding of the house in a merry tune. "I'm just busy right now. I'll let God worry about if it's meant to be, but I don't need anyone. And Heath certainly isn't my type."

"Okay," Tam drawled, "but types change."

Ali bristled. "He's my neighbor, and right now we can hardly get along between fences and bees."

"He's working on it," said Tam.

"Right up until he finishes and goes back to Alabama to teach his classes," Ali reminded her. She wondered why Tam was going on about him. She'd had a good man. A second forever love was not in the cards for her. God had given her a son, and he was enough. She didn't need anyone else, especially the professor across the pasture.

Heath closed his laptop Thursday afternoon, satisfied that the numbers he'd plugged into the spreadsheet tallied perfectly. It gave him a sense of accomplishment, and he pondered over the peculiar satisfaction math gave him when everything aligned. Life he couldn't control, he thought, as he tiptoed through the cluttered hall, but numbers he could manipulate and solve. They were reliable. He tried to ignore the boxes in the kitchen he'd filled with old plastic containers from the cabinets and leaned against the counter to study his to-do list. He was almost sorry he'd eaten a sandwich at his desk, but there was no use in wasting time. Once he finished indoors, he had the outside of the property to deal with, and it could take weeks. He was dreading it. Besides the insurmountable-looking landscaping, there was also the garden to raze and posts and chicken wire to remove. Heath peeked around the door frame and saw Trooper asleep on the couch, so rather than wake him, he set down the list and decided the hall closet would not be too overwhelming a task.

He took a handful of chocolate-covered gummy bears he'd bought at the quirky new bakery in town then grabbed a trash bag to start on the coat closet. When he opened it, a musty cloud of memories disguised as cedar and dust made his nose itch, and he stepped back to let it air out while surrendering to a trio of violent sneezes. As expected, it was crammed with winter jackets, boots and deteriorating boxes on the top shelf. It was a lot to sort out. His stomach sank.

Heath reached up and pulled open the flap of one of the boxes overhead, and a photograph slipped out. It was a picture of him at three years old, standing in the front yard with his father's knit cap pulled over his ears. His cherry-red cheeks glistened from the unseasonably cold temperatures and light dusting of snow. The white powder was something he rarely saw, and his cheesy toddler grin showed how magical it had been to him. Pushing the photo back inside the box, Heath tugged on a puffy dark pink coat until it broke free. He didn't have to put it to his nose to smell his mother. Mental snapshots of her flipped through his mind: Mom walking her dog Beau; cheering at his brother's football game; her face the night they drove Dad to the emergency room for the first time. Heath released a weighted breath and squeezed a bubble of fabric between this thumb and finger. He certainly couldn't wear it, but what should he do? He took it off the hanger, checked the pockets and found a tube of lipstick. His throat knotted again so he folded the coat and set it aside, helpless. The sound of a car pulling into the driveway made him shove the sadness away, and he strolled over to the window to look out. Trooper was on all fours with his nose to the glass, and the dog gave an eager bark, tail wagging.

It was a familiar small blue car, not a delivery driver or Monk. Then up the sidewalk came Ali with the patchwork purse she wore crosswise from her shoulders and a determined look on her face. *Uh-oh.* Heath glanced at the closet and groaned despite the fact he was happy to see another human face, even if it was the beekeeper. Hurrying to the door, he opened it before she could knock, and her eyes rounded in surprise.

"Hello!" She broke into a polite smile. "I hope I'm not interrupting you."

"You're not." Heath waved her in. "Where's Charlie?"

"He doesn't get out of school for two more hours."

Heath returned to the closet to shut it so she didn't see the junk inside, although the room was still stacked with boxes. "I always get the high school and elementary school hours mixed up."

"They changed it around last year so the older kids could sleep in."

Heath chuckled despite himself. "That's not a bad idea. It's why I don't teach morning classes. Nobody shows up."

Ali laughed. "I remember the struggle." She eyed him for a second, then yanked an envelope out of her purse. "Here."

Heath reached out instinctively, and she pushed it into his hand. "What's this?"

"It's for the vet bill."

"You don't have to do that," Heath protested. He tried to give it back.

Ali gave her head a sharp shake of refusal. "I want to. You agreed to pay for half of the survey, and it's likely Trooper was stung by my bees since he was around my property at the time."

Heath would rather she just get rid of them, but he didn't say so. "It's not your fault he was in your yard. I did take down the fence, and he is my dog."

"I understand, but I insist. Maybe if you kept him on a lead or in a pen when he's outside that would help."

"I can't tie him down when I have so much acreage." Heath frowned. "I'm sorry, but it doesn't feel right." He tried to hand the envelope back again, but Ali stepped out of his reach. She set her jaw like she'd screwed it shut with her own stubborn will. "Please," he said, fumbling with the envelope. Inside, he saw layers of twenties. "How about half?" he suggested. "I know you're trying to be a good neighbor, but so am I. Half would be fair, even though I didn't expect it of you."

After a long pause, Ali relented and held out her hand. Heath pulled out the cash and counted it, then gave her half. Her fingers curled around it. "You don't have to worry about everything yourself," he chided her.

She glanced past him. "Isn't that the pot calling the kettle black? I heard some folks at the church offered to help you clean up here, but you refused them."

Heath followed her gaze to the closet. "There's no need for anyone else to see this mess."

"You can't hire a cleaning service?"

"No, I..." He took a deep breath. "I'm trying

to stay on a budget. Plus, I want to make sure nothing important gets thrown away."

Ali gave him an empathetic look, and something about her seemed to soften. "I was blessed to have Tam come to Columbus and help me when the time came for me to deal with my husband's belongings. You really shouldn't have to do this alone."

Heath tried to smile but shrugged instead. "It has to be done, and I'm the only one who can do it with my brother in New Orleans. But the clutter, it's just…" She watched him curiously. "It's a lot," he admitted. "If I didn't have Trooper to take on walks so I can get out of the house and breathe, I think I'd run straight back to Auburn."

"And hide behind your spreadsheets?" she guessed.

Heath wondered how she knew and smiled in surrender. "Yes, and that, too."

Ali tipped her head, and a sliver of sunlight caught the fringes of her hair. It shined like a gemstone, and he tried to decide which one. Ruby? Garnet? Carnelian? "Let me help you."

"What?" Heath snapped out of his deliberations as if caught red-handed.

"I can help you work on that closet until I have to go get Charlie."

"I, uh… It's so messy in there. There might even be some wildlife."

Laughter pealed from Ali, and she smacked the side of her leg. "This is Georgia, Heath. I'm born and bred, and I've seen bugs before. They don't scare me." She walked straight to the closet and yanked out a coat. It was a faded black jacket with a yellow jacket mascot on the left breast pocket. She raised it up along with her brows. "Tech?"

"It was my dad's."

"Makes sense," she replied. She pointed at the embroidered yellow jacket that was crouched and ready to sting. "I didn't think it was yours."

"I'll always be a tiger," he declared.

"That's understandable." She took the jacket off the hanger and cradled it in her arms. "Have you ever worn this?" Heath shook his head no. "And you're not a Tech fan?"

"Right."

Ali held it up again. "I think your dad would understand you wouldn't wear it. It's in pretty rough condition, so I don't think anyone else would want to, either. How about letting it go?"

Heath exhaled with unexpected relief. Her reasoning was more unbiased than his, and it didn't make him feel guilty. "I think you're right." He realized as he said it, the trash bag at his feet was still empty. He was cleaning, but he was also packing everything into boxes as if one of his parents might return. Would he ever finish sorting out the house?

"Tell me about a time you remember him wearing it," Ali invited him. She reached into the closet and pulled a dry cleaning bag from an old dress shirt. Heath stood frozen as his mind reeled backward, and suddenly he was telling her about a Tech ball game he went to with his father. Dad had worn the jacket and let Heath wear his Auburn jersey even though they sat beside the student section in Bobby Dodd Stadium. She laughed, and they moved on to the next hanger after putting the dress shirt in a donation box. One raincoat that had been his was too small, and layers of waterproofing were peeling away. That went into the trash bag without a prick of conscience. Soon, the hangers were empty, and Heath reached for a box on the upper shelf, knowing he was sharing too much, and she probably needed to go.

But he didn't want her to leave. Ali's company made the ordeal seamless and less painful. Her giggles filled the house and lifted some of the weight from his shoulders.

He set a box of baseball cards on the floor as she pulled down a pair of heavy photo albums and sat cross-legged beside him. "Ah, the '70s," she teased. She opened the top album to the first page of sepia-toned photographs where his mom wore bell-bottoms and long hair. A more recent eight-by-ten picture slid out from the back, and Heath's stomach curdled. Ali picked it up before he could reach for it. "Who is this handsome young couple?" she teased with a waggle of her eyebrows.

Heath's face heated, and a bitter taste filled his mouth. "That was my engagement picture," he said, trying to keep his voice steady. He glanced at his younger, starry-eyed self with regret. There was an awkward pause, and Ali set it down.

"I'm sorry." She cleared her throat. "I know this is something you need to deal with alone." Heath picked it up, pretending that the relationship failure did not bother him, while she returned to flipping through the album pages as they sprawled out together on the shag carpeting. Heath studied the picture of Gretchen and himself. Young. In love. But each with different goals that they'd promised to work out. "I think in the back of our minds we each thought the other would compromise," Heath murmured. He looked up and found Ali watching him. "I wanted to go further in school and get my doctorate. She wanted to start living life and move out West because she thought it'd be more exciting. Opposites attract and all that, but we were just different people."

"You said she went to Nevada?"

Heath gave a surly nod. "I should have left with her right away. I could have quit school and gone back later somewhere else."

"Compromise is a two-way street," said Ali. She lifted one side of her lip in a sympathetic smile.

Heath took a deep breath. "Yes. I didn't really have a chance to figure things out or make time to do things her way."

"Then don't be so hard on yourself." Ali turned back to the album. "I admire you for forgiving her. Are you friends?"

Heath started to shake his head then stopped. "Yes. We exchange Christmas cards. It's not unfriendly, but...well, once bitten, twice shy."

"Or stung," Ali agreed with a grimace. "My husband had to do a lot of convincing when we talked about marriage, because I was terrified one of us would change our minds. I need steadiness. Someone to do the scheduling. Because some days I am all over the place." She chuckled. "Your forgiveness says a lot about your character, Heath." Ali gave him a faint smile. "Not to mention, everything you're doing for your parents."

Heath felt like he was falling into her hazel eyes. They were warm. Hypnotic. Safe. He blinked. "Lesson learned," he said, trying to ignore his wandering feelings. "The hard way. The numbers didn't add up with Gretchen, and I ignored that. I won't get stung again." Silence fell over the room, broken only by Trooper's panting. Heath glanced at him. "You're all ears, aren't you, boy?"

Ali climbed to her feet. "I better head over to the school. Charlie will worry if I'm late."

"Sure." Heath joined her, dropping his arms to his sides. He didn't know whether to shake her hand or give her a friendly hug. "Thanks for the assistance," he said instead. "You made this little bit a whole lot easier."

"No problem." Ali smiled. "If you ever want help, I'm happy to do it. I'm terrible at keeping my own house tidy, but I love cleaning other people's homes."

"Thanks." Heath looked down at the baseball cards still on the floor, knowing he couldn't ask someone outside his family to deal with the chaos. "I offered these to Monk to sell so at least they'll have a home."

"I bet they'll go fast," Ali assured him. She gave him a little wave and patted Trooper on her way out.

"Tell Charlie hello for me."

"I will," Ali promised. "He won't be happy he didn't get to come, though. He likes looking through other people's things as much as I do."

Heath chuckled at her honesty as she let herself out the door. Talk about opposites. But this wasn't a math problem. She was just a friend, although he found her as attractive as any other woman who could pull his mind from his spreadsheets. Too bad she already had a family—and a life with her bees.

Chapter Five

Saturday morning, Ali and Charlie wrapped the week's spring vegetables in newspaper and packed them into the car with honey sticks and pint jars of Harding Honey. Glad she split the booth fee with Tam, Ali drove into a glorious sunrise. It shot arrows of light across the county until she reached a primitive gas station that sold fuel, bait and soda at a crossroads. Swinging a left past an old cemetery, she listened to Charlie prattle about marlin fishing.

The boy was clueless about how her guts writhed every time she passed a cemetery, but she knew she was strong enough to keep living her life. What was hard was watching her son grow up the past four years without his dad around. She pined quietly for a few minutes, then forced her attention to the wildflowers waving from the ditches on either side of the road.

She was thankful for her foundation of faith that had supported her hope of the Resurrection and eternity when it was sorely tested; it was just lonely without someone at her side, and when she let herself think about it, the pain came back. Their little family felt incomplete, and as hard as she tried to honor Keith's memory, it wasn't fulfilling their lives in the way Ali expected.

The road widened, and she merged into the center lane and turned left into the gravel parking area of the county farmers market. It was really an aggrandized bazaar where an old wooden barn had been replaced by an enormous concrete pad with a steel roof. Some vendors had set up canopies in neat rows north of the shelter, giving off art festival airs, and food trucks bordered the edges of the property with tempting treats.

Ali shut off the car, and Charlie jumped out to unload the vegetables before she could, insisting that he was strong enough. Tam was already at their booth when they walked in under the breezeway and waved. "Good morning! Charlie, I have a surprise for you!" she called.

Charlie deposited the vegetables rather roughly to the ground, and Ali winced. He darted over, and Tam offered him a small container, which he opened with delight. Ali peeked inside when she reached them. "Doughnut holes? Really, Tam?"

"I already ate mine." Ten-year-old Piper Rochester gave her short, bobbed hair a toss, unaware she had powdered sugar on her chin. Ali tsked but couldn't stop a smile.

"Wow! Thank you!" cried Charlie. He gave his mother a gleeful peek and darted past her, shoving a doughnut into his mouth.

"Oh, Ali, a little sugar now and then doesn't hurt a boy," Tam reminded her.

Ali began stacking her honey beside a small chalkboard that listed her items and prices. "And you own a health food store," she groused.

Tam snorted. "It's across the road from the Last Re-Torte Bakery, which you happen to appreciate as much as I do. Do you know how hard it is to look across a street at cakes all day long? Sometimes I can smell the sugar through the window!" She motioned toward the next table, selling antique children's toys, which Charlie was examining with Piper at his side. "Piper just had to go investigate the menu this morning, and I ended up buying an apple fritter. The doughnut holes were buy three, get three. I thought it'd fuel him up."

"It'll fuel him up, all right," Ali groaned, although she didn't really mind. She knew not having a treat now and then would only make her son go overboard when he had the opportunity. She held up the honey sticks she'd made the day before. "What do you think? Samples to get my name out there?"

Tam pursed her lips and slipped one out of Ali's fingers. "I think your name is pretty well-known, at least locally, but these are a great idea."

"Slowly but surely." Ali took a breath of determination. "I'd like to get into stores someday, but that's a long way off."

"You just keep me supplied for now," Tam tutted. "How are the new hives?"

"The third and fourth have their bees, so it shouldn't be too long now."

They sat down together behind their table, and Ali chose a honey stick flavored with orange essential oil to keep her mouth busy as Tam's first customer of the day asked about alternative recommendations for antacids. Ali tapped her fingers, biting her tongue so she didn't butt in with a honey-based remedy, but she offered the gentleman a free honey stick as Tam wrapped up his herbal purchase. When Tam sat down, a cool breeze riffled over them, and Charlie shot by. "Hi, Mom. Bye, Mom."

"Don't go far, honeybee," Ali called after him. Charlie skidded to a stop a few yards away to watch a yo-yo expert do some tricks.

"Tell Piper to come check in with me," ordered Tam. The smell of sausage biscuits carried on the breeze. Tam inhaled and sighed.

"That smells delicious," Ali agreed.

"It won't be long until the popcorn machine's running," said Tam. "That I can't resist."

Ali hummed in agreement, then held out honey sticks for Sister Lovell and a friend wearing matching embroidered capri pants after they approached the table. They each thanked her. Sister Lovell examined Ali's produce that was arranged in baskets and neat rows. "Do I smell sausage?" asked her friend. Tam pointed at one of the food trucks in the parking lot. Sister Lovell grinned with mischief and looped her arm through her friend's and tugged her away. "I'll be back for the radishes," she promised Ali. "Set some aside? I'll pay up later."

Ali nodded and reached over the table to choose a good bunch. "So did you pay up on Trooper's vet bill?" Tam wondered while Ali wrapped the radishes in an eco-friendly bag.

"I tried." Ali sat back in her camp chair as the morning breeze fluttered through her bangs. She swept them out of her eyes. "I went to his house and found him cleaning out a closet like it was a tomb."

"I bet."

"I mean it was crammed, and he was pretty solemn. At first."

"What'd he say about the money?"

"He'd only accept half for it, and I had to talk him into it."

"That was gentlemanly," Tam pointed out. "Your bottom line is going to be tight until the honey is ready, anyway."

"That's true. I'm sure he's trying to be neighborly and all, but I know what he really wants."

Tam's eyes narrowed. "What does he want?"

"For me to get rid of my bees!" Ali grumbled. "He isn't even going to be here after the summer, but he acts like my land is as much a hazard as his parents' place."

Tam twirled a honey stick through her fingers and watched people pass by as rays of sunshine stretched farther across the concrete. Somewhere, a rooster crowed, then a dog barked. "You're not going anywhere with a home paid for and a new business, and he's obviously not going to sell that property, so you're going to have to make it work until he rents the house out."

"That's why I offered to help," Ali admitted. She thought about the old photo album. "He had a bunch of pictures to go through. The Underwoods look like they were a good family. Close. It's really sad."

"It's too bad he's lost both his parents now."

"And his only brother lives far away," added Ali. "He has no other relatives around, and I think that bothers him. I found an old engagement photo that his mother had held on to for some reason."

"Of hers?"

"No, of Heath and his wife. He was in the middle of finishing his doctorate so he could teach at the university level, and she had a change of heart about supporting him and moved to Nevada. He'd planned to make arrangements to get out there, but she found someone else in the meantime, so he had to let her go."

"Wow," drawled Tam. "That's a lot."

"Yes, and I can tell it scarred him. He's definitely a man that stays the course, so I don't know why she couldn't wait a little longer. It definitely blindsided him."

"Sometimes you don't see it coming." Tam's eyes clouded.

Ali knew she was thinking of her ex-fiancé and reached over and rested a hand on her leg. "He wanted you to be happy."

"I know," said Tam with an echo of bitterness. "He also wanted to go to Chicago and play cops and robbers without me."

"He just wasn't ready for a family."

Tam sighed. "I know, but I was. Still am. And here I sit because he couldn't bring himself to propose and wanted to live the bachelor life in a big city."

"He's doing what he loves, and he loves you,"

Ali assured her. "Sometimes things just don't click." Tam nodded, blinking away misty tears. "I'm glad I have you," whispered Ali. She decided to change the subject. "You get on me about moving on," she pointed out. "What about you?"

"I try," said Tam defensively. "I have Piper and a business to run, too, you know." She sucked on a honey straw and turned her attention to the crowd, so Ali let it go. They were both strong women, and they had each other. She knew it was all *she* needed. She tidied her honey jars as a couple with a small child approached the table.

"I hear honey is good for allergies," said the woman with interest. She motioned toward her little girl. "She has terrible hay fever."

"Local honey is exactly what you need." Ali rose to her feet. She handed the woman a small jar and went through her sales pitch.

"I don't know," drawled the husband beside her. "I think shots would do just as well."

"If it's serious," Ali relented, "but you can't beat a natural remedy if it takes care of your needs." The man gave her a doubtful stare.

"And it makes a good salve, too," someone interjected. Ali looked over in surprise. Heath stood beside the table with a sparkle in his eye. He grinned at her customers and pulled the salve Ali had given him from his pocket. "I had a spider bite two days ago, and it's almost gone." He held out his arm and showed it to them.

Ali examined it along with the potential customers. "Cleaning out closets again?"

Heath nodded cheerfully. "Yep."

"What kind of spider was it?" asked the man in a suspicious tone.

"Nothing deadly, but it itched pretty bad the first day. The salve eased that and stopped the swelling."

"Hmm," said Doubting Thomas.

"It has tea tree, peppermint and lavender oils in it," Ali explained.

"Interesting. Okay, I'll try one," the woman decided. "And some honey, too."

Ali shot Heath a look of gratitude, then bagged up the purchases while Tam chatted with everyone. As the couple meandered away with a pint jar of honey, Ali crossed her arms. "For someone who has a problem with bees, you sure are helping me with sales," she said to Heath.

He shrugged. "The salve did help, I'll give you that." He examined the table with his hands on his hips. "Is this all the honey you have?"

Ali nodded. "I only have a few jars left at home until the first harvest at the end of the summer. I'm running pretty low."

"What are you here for today?" wondered

Tam as the rooster in the distance crowed again. "Chickens?"

Heath chuckled. "No. I don't think Trooper and chickens would get on well." He wrapped Trooper's lead around his wrist and pulled the dog closer. Trooper dropped to his haunches to wait patiently beside him.

Ali couldn't help but smile at the adoring dog who seemed to listen to every word of their conversation. She offered her hand for him to investigate, then patted him lovingly on the head after he licked her fingers.

"Actually, I'm here with Monk Coles," Heath explained. He pointed over his shoulder. Sure enough, at the end of the pavilion, the robust man from church was in his trademark overalls selling his various collectibles while Charlie talked his ears off.

"Monk has puppies, I understand," said Tam.

"That he does."

Ali groaned. "He told Charlie about them at the church potluck. I hope he's not trying to sell them today."

"He's not, just his stuff and mine."

"You brought your things over?" Ali scanned Monk's table.

Heath nodded. "The baseball cards and some of my dad's models." His voice caught just as

Monk walked up with his wife, Angie, at his side. Charlie was at their heels.

"Mom! Mr. Monk has an antique honey pot."

Ali feigned surprise. "Is that so?"

"Yes, and Mr. Heath is selling his ship."

"Just a model, I hope," Ali teased.

Charlie laughed. "Yes. Old Ironsides."

"Good morning, you two." Ali greeted Monk and Angie with a smile. "How's your morning going?"

Monk thumbed his overall straps. "It's going well so far. We sold a collection of china Angie has been holding on to forever, and I'm glad she did. How's the honey business?"

"Slow, but it's coming along." Ali slid a glance toward Heath. "I just set up our twenty-eighth hive, so by next year I should be able to keep up with demand and grow even more."

"That's wonderful news." Monk motioned toward Heath with a curled pinkie. "Heath is letting me sell some of his parents' things."

"His mother had beautiful collections," said Angie.

Heath's smile tightened, and Ali grinned because she knew he saw most of it as junk that his conscience wouldn't allow him to toss. "He was just telling us about it," said Ali. "I'm glad they're going to people who'll appreciate them."

"Are you staying all day, Heath?" Tam asked.

"Not today, although I think I'd enjoy hanging out here a few hours on Saturday mornings." Heath turned to Monk. "I feel like I should help."

"You're always welcome, but don't worry about it if you have things to do. If your stuff draws people to my tables, then it's worth it to me."

"But you won't take an equal split," Heath groused.

"I think twenty-five percent is more than fair," said Monk. "Don't be so generous. I thought you were a numbers man." He slapped Heath on the back.

Heath chuckled, and Ali realized he was proud of his profession. It was the property and the untidy house that seemed to embarrass him. "I am, but I like to be fair."

Ali opened her mouth to tell everyone he'd generously agreed to split the cost of the land survey but changed her mind. Instead she said to him, "The surveyor is coming out Monday."

Heath glanced down at Trooper then met Ali's eyes. "What time?"

"Between lunchtime and two in the afternoon. That'll give me time before I have to pick up Charlie from school."

"Let me know when they get there," Heath reminded her. "I can come out and stay with them if you have to leave."

"Thanks." She smiled, but feeling Tam's watchful gaze on her, let it fade.

"It's nice of you to split the cost of the survey," said Tam.

"It's the neighborly thing to do," Heath insisted.

Monk scratched his chin and looked from Heath to Ali for an explanation. "What are you getting the land surveyed for?"

Heath shuffled his feet. "I took down the back fence before checking to see whose property it was on," he admitted.

"And I'd really like to have a fence back there," finished Ali.

"Good fences make good neighbors," chirped Angie. Her husband elbowed her.

"Right," agreed Ali. "They keep animals out of my hives." She might as well have said Trooper's name, the way Heath exhaled then cleared his throat loudly. "How many bees is that now with two more hives?" he queried.

Ali bit the inside of her bottom lip as Charlie answered for her. "There's an average of sixty thousand bees in a beehive," he announced. "I know because I'm doing a bee experiment for my science project."

"Goodness, and you have how many hives in all?" asked Angie, surprised.

"Twenty-eight," said Ali, darting a peek at

Heath. "I plan to have thirty by the end of the summer." She watched his Adam's apple bob in his throat as he swallowed. Gulped, actually.

"That's well over a million bees," he observed. "One million, eight hundred..." His last few words sounded wheezy.

"It takes twelve bees to make a teaspoon of honey," Charlie elucidated. "So you need a lot. We're going to have one hundred hives before I turn ten." He held up both hands and wiggled all his fingers.

"Wow." Heath looked serious, and Ali knew she should have mentioned her long-term goal of owning two hundred–plus hives to have a commercial business someday, but before she could explain, he took a step back. "Thanks for taking care of the baseball cards today, Monk. Let me know if there's anything else I can do for you."

Monk waved him off. "Don't give it another thought. In fact, you should let some of us from the church come over and give you a hand with all that landscaping you need done in the yard. I know you have a lot on your plate."

Heath flushed but shook his head. "No, it's fine. I can do it. I should have done more when I came up after Mom got sick."

"It's not that bad," Ali said carefully.

"It's bad enough. I'm glad someone's finally going to do something about it." Sister Lovell had arrived to pick up her radishes, and Ali wanted to toss them at her.

"Yes, I know it's in bad shape," said Heath abruptly.

"I'm happy to help out some more," Ali offered.

"I can handle it. Look, I'll see y'all later. I need to get back to the house."

"Here." Ali offered Heath a honey stick. He gave her a plastic-looking smile and shook his head, pulling Trooper after him and looking put out. Ali hoped it wasn't because he'd just learned about her future plans.

They watched him go as a group, and Monk said, "It's hard to believe he's back home, but I'm glad." He rocked back on his boot heels. "We were really sorry when he divorced that girl from Natchez. Shame."

"He's divorced now?" Sister Lovell chimed in. "His poor mother." Ali shoved the bag of radishes into her hands, hoping she'd move along. "She sure left those boys a mess to deal with at her house."

Monk turned to Ali. "I'll have a pint of your honey, Ali, and please let us know when you start selling in bulk. That'd be more convenient."

"It's going to be a while," Ali admitted.

"Who needs more than a pint jar at a time?"

wondered Sister Lovell as she accepted her change.

Ali bulged her eyes at Tam and sank into her chair when the woman finally disappeared. Monk saw it, and the corners of his mouth twitched. "Don't take her personally, Ali, or Heath, either," he soothed her.

"I've offered to help Heath, so I try not to," she said carefully.

He rested his arms on his generous belly. "Hoarding stresses a lot of people out. He always was a careful, orderly boy." Monk's tone was tender. "I'm sure losing parents and a spouse in the span of several years while trying to build a career takes its toll on a person."

"He just needs a little push," said Tam. "I think he's lonely being away from his university, and no one in Lagrasse should be lonely."

Monk back looked toward his booth. "I can invite him to come out every Saturday morning. Trooper seemed to have a good time."

Ali flinched at the thought of Heath a few tables down from her every weekend. He'd see her selling her honey and beeswax products, which would remind him of bees, and that would naturally take him back to his childhood calamity. She didn't like the idea of Heath being uncomfortable around her, but what could she do? "He probably needs the weekends to work on his yard," she blustered. The truth was, it'd be better if he finished working on his parents' house and hurried back to school. Tam gave her a shifty glance.

"Mom!" Charlie raced up, breaking the awkward interlude. He held a baseball card. "Look what Mr. Heath gave me! For free!"

Chapter Six

Heath braced himself for looks of surprise when he slunk into the sanctuary on Sunday morning, but no one seemed to notice him. He tiptoed in and sat at the end of a row where sunlight streamed through the stained glass, draping the floor and the corner of a pew in puddles of blue. He found himself breathing slowly and deeply, a cleansing act that made him relax as the pastor talked about God closing doors and opening windows. The rainbow light from the window had crept to his feet, and Heath felt a rush of air as the air conditioner kicked on overhead after the last *amen*. When the choir stood in colorful red robes and sang an inspiring version of "Battle Hymn of the Republic," his spirit felt lighter and renewed.

Angie Coles looked over her shoulder from the second row after he stood, and she grinned as if she was excited to see him. That wasn't unusual, but after a few warm greetings from old friends and a sister who'd been his Sunday school teacher when he was twelve, Heath decided no one was thinking about the Underwood house in shambles or that he'd left home married and returned again alone. Except for Sister Lovell, maybe. He sidestepped chattering people to make his escape, but before he reached the lobby, there was a tug on the back of his shirt. To his surprise, Heath found Charlie standing behind him in a short-sleeved white shirt and bow tie with approval in his dark eyes. "You're at church," the boy stated.

"I am."

"Is this your church, too?" asked Charlie.

"It is. I just haven't been in a long time." Heath offered his hand, and, pleased to be treated like a peer, Charlie shook it.

"Use your other hand," Heath suggested. "We always shake with our right hands."

Charlie furrowed his brow and stared at both of his palms as if trying to remember which was which. "How do you know?"

"My dad taught me," said Heath, then he remembered Charlie was fatherless. "Or maybe it was my grandpa, but it's something that has to be learned."

"Oh." Nonplussed, Charlie stuck out the correct hand, and they shook properly.

"Very good." Heath smiled. "Win or lose, a gentleman always shakes hands."

"We're going to have a science fair at school, and it's going to be fun. First place gets a trophy, and I'm going to win it."

"I like your enthusiasm," Heath approved. "I wanted to work in a laboratory with microscopes before I decided I liked math better."

"Are you going to work in the woods tomorrow, or are you going to clean your house?" wondered Charlie.

"I'm not sure," Heath admitted. "I have to teach my classes, and if I have time I need to run a load to the donation center."

Charlie made a face. "That doesn't sound like fun. Don't you ever have time to swing?"

Heath chuckled. "If I decide to work out back, I'll send Trooper to find you."

"Good idea!" exclaimed Charlie, then his eyes rounded. "Wait. You mean he knows how to fetch people?"

"I don't know," teased Heath, "but I bet he could learn."

"Can he catch a Frisbee?"

"Yes. He's pretty good."

"That's neat. I wish I could have a dog. Did you know Mr. Monk has dogs?"

"Yes," said Heath. "He told me all about them."

"What about Monk's dogs?" Ali appeared out of nowhere in a dark pink skirt that swished around her calves. She wore a white sweater with a green paisley scarf around her neck, and the pleasing picture made Heath's stomach drop. Her cheeks and lips were dusted with something pink, and it made the green in her eyes glow. Tongue-tied, Heath was relieved when Charlie filled her in.

"I was just telling Mr. Heath that Mr. Monk has dogs."

Heath looked at him fondly. "You can call me Heath and drop the mister now."

"Oh, no," Ali cut in. "I want him to show proper respect to adults outside of our family."

Heath shrugged with a smile, although something pricked his heart. "Mr. Heath it is."

Charlie gave his mother a scowl, then turned to Heath. "At least I don't have to call your dog, *Mr.* Trooper."

Ali gave him the stink eye, and the boy ran off. "I'm sorry," Heath said, as people brushed past them to file out the door. "I thought we knew each other well enough."

"It's okay," Ali assured him. "He thinks you're wonderful, but I want to raise him the way I was raised. Hopefully, it will pay off in the long run."

"I'm sure it will," Heath agreed. "I did have to show him how to shake hands, though. He used the wrong hand."

"I never thought of that." Ali's friendly smile melted away. "There are a lot of things that don't always fall under a mother's purview that I don't think to do."

Heath felt her heartache. Not only had he lost a spouse, but he'd also lost his father and missed that influence. "I'm happy to help out with anything Charlie needs," he offered. "I think I'll show him how to play Frisbee with Trooper."

"I'm not sure he knows how to throw a Frisbee, either," Ali admitted. "Thanks. I'm sure he'd love that, and I appreciate it with everything you have going on." She looked around the room as if wanting to avoid looking into his eyes, then raised her hand and waved at a woman dragging her husband out the door. When she looked back, Heath saw a shimmer in her eyes that hinted at emotion. "You really don't have to do it unless you want to."

"I don't mind." Heath gave her a steady stare, aware of a new depth in his heartbeat. He enjoyed being around Charlie. He enjoyed being around Ali. With the exception of her peculiar vocation, he liked her very much. Something fluttered across his chest like a bird in motion. Heath took a step back. What was this persistent sensation of being awakened—of feeling at home—whenever Ali walked into view? He was getting drawn in, not to Charlie, but to something more. Ali was not his type; she was a mother, and for heaven's sake, the woman kept bees. Millions of them. "I should go," Heath pardoned himself. "Trooper will be wanting his walk."

Ali nodded in agreement. "I better go see where Charlie ran off to, or I may end up with one of Monk's puppies."

Heath chuckled as she rushed out, pulling the strap of her purse over her petite shoulder. When she stepped through the door into the sunlight, her red hair brightened and shined like the stained glass windows in the sanctuary. Heath wondered what it would be like to curl a lock around his finger, then jumped when a hand landed on his shoulder. "Heath," exclaimed Angie Coles. "We're so happy you're here!" And for the first time in years, Heath was happy to be there.

The surveyor called at lunchtime on Monday, and Ali listened for a vehicle to pull into the driveway while she picked up the house. When the doorbell rang, she found a man with a tripod and duffel bag under his arm, and she escorted him to the backyard. Mr. Giles was a nice man, and he seemed to understand her predicament after seeing the apiary. When they reached the ditch where the fence had been, Ali offered him a bottle of water, but he shook his head.

"I keep some in my truck," he explained, "but thank you."

"Then I'll let you get to work." Ali hoped she sounded agreeable. She searched the trees edging the Underwoods' property and saw a ribbon of smoke. It looked like there was a fire, and she wondered what was burning. "I forgot to call my neighbor and tell him you were here," she told Mr. Giles. "I'll be right back." Treading through trees now fully dressed in thick, green leaves, she found lacy ferns and a carpet of wild violets blooming in purple clusters in the shade. The beauty almost calmed her blustery nerves, but she was still on edge. If the fence was on her side, she'd have to pressure Heath to put up another one, but she knew he already had plenty to do, and he was on a budget, too. She had no idea how much the fence would cost. Ali sighed. Adulting *was* hard and never seemed to get any easier.

When she emerged from the woods, she found Heath at a burn pile, poking it with a long stick. He wore casual shorts that hit the top of his knee and a fitted nylon shirt with a collar that made him look ready for the golf course. Trooper noticed her, barked in delight, then bounded up for a scratch behind the ears. Heath raised his hand in polite greeting. Ali gave Trooper a firm pat on the back. "Come," she beckoned, and he followed her to his master, who'd returned to tending the flames. There was a large bucket of water beside a lawn chair and a bottle of bug spray. "Are you camping out now?" she teased.

Heath chuckled. "No. It's tempting with all the dust in the house, but the mosquitoes are out."

"It's never too early for them, it seems. What are you burning?"

"Just sticks and weeds I pulled from the flower beds this morning."

Ali wondered if there were photographs in the fire, too, but didn't ask. "I'm happy to make a run to the recycling center if you need me to," she offered as ashes floated through the air.

"Thanks, but we do have a recycling can. It's just full of magazines and shoeboxes right now. I don't mind burning brush until the burn ban goes into effect."

"Oh." A nice spring breeze danced over them, partnering with the smoke and leading it away so that the air filled with sweetness. "Have you heard from the county again?"

Heath shook his head. "No. I hope they can see I'm cleaning things up around here. We had two old cars in the side yard towed right after the funeral, and my brother trimmed some of the hedges about a month before I came up."

"It's already a great deal better," said Ali. "I think what you've done so far looks good, and they can't see what you've done inside. When is your semester over?"

"Near the end of May." Heath stabbed the fire again with the stick. His forearm was muscular, smooth and brown. "I'm ready to get started outside sooner than I expected, but…there's a lot to do."

And a lot of bees and other stinging insects, Ali guessed. "I'm sure you'll have time to get the house on the market by the end of the summer," she encouraged him. "You should consider letting volunteers from the church help."

Heath crouched and stirred some embers. "I'm going to miss it here more than I realized. It's nice being home for the most part."

Ali assumed he meant despite the bees, and she tensed. "It's been nice having a new neighbor. I mean, I never knew your parents, but…"

"I know what you meant." Heath looked at her curiously.

"I'm sorry I didn't go out of my way to get to know your mother better," Ali said with sincerity.

"You had a lot going on in your life, losing a husband and moving to a new town. I'm sure she understood."

"I should have made more effort, though." Ali searched the sky as if it held reminders of more regrets then she remembered the fence. "Oh. I came over to tell you the surveyor is here, but it slipped my mind."

Heath stood up and stretched. "I didn't realize it was so late already."

"No worries, and it's not. He's early, actually." She gave Heath a meek smile. "I saw the smoke from the fire and wanted to make sure everything was okay."

"It's fine, thanks." Heath tamped the edges of the burn pile, then dumped water from the bucket over it. After it steamed away, he checked it one more time, called for Trooper and together they followed Ali into the woods. He pointed out the tree house, and she showed him the flowers. When they reached the furrow between their yards, Mr. Giles was packing up his things like he was finished.

"Mr. Giles," called Ali. "How does it look?"

"I'll send you the official report in a couple weeks," he answered, dusting off his hands. Trooper jumped up on him, and Heath called him back.

"It's fine," said Mr. Giles. He gave Trooper a good scratch behind the ears.

"He knows better," said Heath. "Trooper, sit."

The dog plopped onto his hindquarters immediately. Ali chuckled as a stream of doubt trickled through her. She wanted a fence up, but was it really a necessity? Charlie enjoyed going into the small patch of trees on Heath's land and talking with him. And then there was the tree house and the swing. She glanced toward the garden and apiary. However, there was the bee issue, and Trooper had already been stung.

She prodded Mr. Giles again. "What do you think?" Beside her, Heath took a step away as if to draw an invisible line between them. A dragonfly darted by, then decided to take a nosedive toward him. The man hopped back again like an elephant had stepped on his toe, and Ali saw a flash of panic on his face before he realized what it was. "It's just a dragonfly," she said calmly.

"I see that," Heath replied, sounding embarrassed. His handsome blue eyes clouded.

Mr. Giles looked at them oddly, then shrugged it off. "I could hear your bees while I was working. It's relaxing. I'll have to try some of your honey."

"You're welcome to a sample," Ali offered. She avoided Heath's gaze.

"So about the fence," Heath began. "I mean, the property line. Can you tell us where it is?"

"It looks like it's almost where the old fence was," said Mr. Giles.

"Almost?" asked Ali with bated breath. She reminded herself to keep things in perspective.

"The fence was just past your property line," Mr. Giles said to Ali. "To be precise, it appears it was on the Underwoods' land by six inches."

A stream of disappointment coursed through

her, and Ali sneaked a peek at Heath. He seemed nonplussed, and to her surprise, his expression of anticipation changed into one of regret. "I was right, then. I really did believe my grandpa put it up." Was he sorry he'd been right? Ali bit the inside of her cheek in amazement.

"It makes sense," said Mr. Giles. "Your home is older. I remember when all this was farmland." He waved the tip of his tripod in the air. "I'm sorry, Mrs. Harding."

"It's okay." Ali forced herself to offer a smile of surrender. If she wanted a fence, she'd have to put one up herself, but there was simply no money for it right now.

Heath put his hands on his hips and studied her. "I can't say I'm not relieved with everything I have to do already, but maybe we can talk about another compromise later."

Appreciating his futile goodwill, Ali nodded mutely.

"I should get going for my next appointment," said Mr. Giles. He shook Ali's hand and turned to Heath. "I remember your father. We went to high school together."

Ali watched Heath's eyes light up, the fence forgotten. "You did?"

"Yes, he was a good man."

"Thank you," said Heath. "It's nice to know he's not forgotten."

"He's not," Mr. Giles assured him. "I miss seeing him at the football games. He kept coming even after your brother graduated." His long jowls stretched into a grin. "And at the farmers market on the weekends. Your mom and him were always looking to buy one thing or another."

Ali grinned before she could stop herself. "I believe Heath is going to follow in his footsteps. He was there this past weekend."

Heath gave a tight smile. "Yes, to sell, not to buy. But I enjoyed it more than I should have, especially with all the work I need to do around here."

Mr. Giles nodded. "I'm sorry for your losses. I know it can be tough moving on without your parents—I've been there myself."

Heath's friendly expression faded, and he lowered his gaze to the ground. Ali appreciated Mr. Giles sharing his sympathies. Heath needed to know he wasn't the only person to go through the trauma of losing family. There were other painful things in life besides bee stings. Suddenly, the fence didn't seem important.

"Thank you," murmured Heath. "I'm sure they would have appreciated the kind words. I do." They shook hands.

As Mr. Giles started off, Heath walked up to Ali, his gaze flitting toward the hives. He let out a heavy breath. "So I guess you'd like me to put a fence back up." Trooper barked then rushed into the trees like he'd been summoned, and they were left alone. Since she was standing so close to him, Ali reached for Heath's hand. She wasn't certain if it was to assure him she wasn't angry or because she wanted to hold it. His fingers brushed hers and sent a warm current up her arm. Jolted, she let go and inched away. Heath was a nice man married to his career, but despite his kindness and goodness, he was making her anxious about her bees, and she couldn't afford that. "Don't worry about it," she stammered. "I'll just put one up myself when I can." The hives were her future, and she couldn't afford to relent or slow down. "I better go," she excused herself. They were spending entirely too much time together. "I have work to do, too."

"On the hives?" Heath's tone sounded controlled.

"Yes, and in the garden," replied Ali. "I have to keep up with payments on a business loan, and Charlie's trip means everything to him. I can't go into any more debt with my house on the line."

"I didn't know you could lose your home if you lost your business." Heath made a peculiar face. "Do you need an accountant?"

"No," said Ali hurriedly. "I can figure it out

myself." She didn't admit she might have to put some of April's payment on her only credit card, even though she needed it for Charlie's trip.

"I'll let you get back to your bees, then."

"They really are harmless," Ali found herself saying. "So am I." She could have sworn Heath flushed at that, and she cringed when he waved goodbye. Was she flirting? She hadn't done anything like that in a long time, and why would she? Ali hoped Heath knew she only meant to be friendly.

On her way to the house, Trooper tried to follow her, and she shooed him off until they heard the sound of his master's voice calling. "Go on now, Troop," she scolded the dog. "You don't want to get stung again, do you?"

Trooper whined in his throat, then took off running toward Heath's voice, and Ali sighed with relief. She didn't want the dog to get hurt again. She didn't want any more problems with Heath, and despite the cost, it'd be best if she replaced the old fence as soon as possible. She needed something between Heath and herself, because Trooper might have a worse allergic reaction if he was stung again. Her heart drooped, but she told herself it was because of her concern for the dog.

Chapter Seven

Tuesday afternoon, Heath did more yard work and hauled the wheelbarrow of clippings to the fire pit, although he didn't have time to burn them. The next day, he made a second trip and started a fire, peering through the trees and wondering if Ali would show up again. She'd only walked over before to tell him about Mr. Giles's arrival. It'd been presumptuous of him to take down the fence without checking into it properly first. Thankfully, his pretty neighbor had been willing to do things right and bore no grudge that things hadn't gone her way. He dropped into the lawn chair beside the small fire. He didn't want wire fencing. Wood was his preference, but it was a lot more expensive. He crumpled a tissue from his pocket and threw it into the flames.

Despite the shocking number of hives she managed, Ali had been more than understanding about his feelings. Their initial run-in had been awkward, but she was a good person. His first impression had been of an overly assertive, business-obsessed, protective mother, but she'd turned out to be nothing more than a polite, straightforward woman who loved animals and liked the same music he did. She was just trying to build a business while caring for her little boy. Heath could relate. He had a job to keep, a property to maintain, and although he didn't have a sweet little boy like Charlie, there was Trooper.

Remembering his dog, Heath searched the tree line and gave a shrill whistle. After a pause, he called, "Trooper! Here, boy!" The brush in the distance rattled, and Trooper burst out with Charlie at his heels. The little boy had to sprint to keep up with the dog, and he gave Heath a wide, toothy grin when he reached him out of breath. "Hi, Mr. Heath!" he panted.

"Hi, Charlie."

"What are you burning?"

Heath stirred the stick around. "Just some weeds."

"Is there any poison ivy? I got poison ivy last year and itched forever."

"No," said Heath. "But there are blackberry stems. They have very sharp thorns."

"I hope you don't get stabbed," said Charlie with concern. "I stepped on a stinger kettle without my shoes on once, and my foot swolled up this big." He spread his hands out in an exaggerated motion the size of a beach ball.

Heath thumbed through a mental glossary of native plants. "I think you mean stinging nettle," he suggested.

Charlie shrugged and watched the fire crawl from plant stalk to plant stalk. "I stepped on a bee once, too."

"Did you?" Heath shuddered in empathy. For a mother who was so protective, Ali certainly didn't seem to be concerned her little boy could get stung. "Were you okay? That can be dangerous." Trooper yipped in agreement.

"It only hurt a little." Charlie cast an adoring look at Trooper, who jogged in circles around them like he was in a circus. "I should have been wearing my shoes, but I forgot." Charlie dropped to his knees and stared at the flames, mesmerized. "Can I stir the fire?"

"Sure." Heath handed him the scorched stick he'd been using, and the boy took it with eager hands. "How was school today?"

"Fine."

"Do you like it? I'm a teacher, and I like school."

"I like it some of the time," Charlie admitted. He cast Heath a serious glance. "Except I don't like homework."

"Me, either," Heath commiserated, "but it

helps us learn new things." Trooper barked and ran for the trees. Heath watched him go then turned back to Charlie. "Do you have friends?"

"I have two friends. Darren and Justice."

"That's nice. Friends are important, huh?"

"Yes. Do teachers have friends?"

The question caught Heath off guard. He paused, mind groping for a reply. "I have... Trooper. He's my friend."

"I'm your friend, too," Charlie said as if he felt sorry for him.

"I have lots of friends," Heath replied, somewhat defensively. "There're hundreds of students in my classes."

"When are you going back?"

"After the summer."

"Who's going to live there?" Charlie pointed toward Heath's house.

"I don't know," Heath admitted.

"I hope they like bees."

"I hope they're not allergic," Heath said.

"I wonder if they'll like tree houses, too." Charlie sounded wistful.

Heath studied him, and the boy shifted his eyes back to the flames. "You weren't at the tree house, were you?"

Charlie's face colored, but he grinned innocently. "We have a ladder in the kitchen." Then he met Heath's eyes with some uncertainty. "I brought it outside to see if I could get up there."

Heath tried to suppress a smile. "Do you remember I told you it wasn't safe?"

"You said it *probably* wasn't. I checked. It's safe."

"I think a grown-up should have a look first. It's really old."

"I didn't get hurt."

Heath reached for the stick as Charlie climbed to his feet. The tip of it glowed. "Did you get up inside?"

"Yes." The boy hung his head.

Heath sighed. He couldn't risk Ali's son getting hurt because he hadn't taken the tree house down. "Your mom—"

"Only some of the boards are rotten," blurted Charlie. "I threw them on the ground. I threw off all the black square things, too."

"The shingles?" Heath realized Charlie had begun something he should have taken care of himself, and that there was now a pile of trash at the bottom of the sprawling tree. "Did you get poked by any nails?"

"No," Charlie promised. "I can see your house from there," he continued, glowing like the moon. Then it waned. "I'm really careful. Don't tell my mom."

A laugh spurted from Heath's mouth before he

could stop it. He pretended to cough and reached for the bucket of water he'd brought to put out the fire. Charlie watched in fascination as it gurgled and hissed, and when it quieted, Heath stuck out his hand. "Come on," he said. "Let's go have a look at your work. But we'll have to tell your mom because that's the right thing to do."

Charlie's face crumpled, but he took Heath's hand, and they trudged across the pasture, stopping only to take a Frisbee from Trooper. Heath showed Charlie how to throw it. After a few successful tosses, they continued to the tree house, where a small utility stepladder leaned against the beech's trunk.

Heath looked up. Charlie must have been able to just reach the top foothold and scramble up with his feet. "You're quite the little squirrel, aren't you?" Heath murmured, looking around. Debris was all over the place. Stepping up the ladder, he pulled himself to the platform and swung a leg over. After patting around to make sure it was stable, he heaved himself over the top of it. Charlie was right behind him and needed no assistance. Heath stayed seated for safety's sake and examined the structure for rot. The roof was pretty much gone, and a few pieces of the platform were disintegrating, but the suspicious-looking supports were actually holding strong. It was not in as bad a condition as he'd initially thought. Charlie hiked one foot up onto the barrel-thick tree trunk and scanned the woods like he was in a crow's nest.

"I could fix this up if you wanted," offered Heath.

"Can you?" Charlie asked hopefully. He started to skip around. "That would be awesome!"

"Awesome?" Heath's mouth twitched.

"It means like…like really great." Charlie's bottom lip sucked in. "Like at school when we have pizza, we say lunch is awesome."

So a tree house would be awesome. Heath chuckled and sat back against the trunk, soaking in the fresh air. It hummed a promising tune of summertime, freedom, happiness. He felt safe. His mind flooded with memories he'd made in this very tree. "Maybe on days when I get finished early in the yard, we can come out here and work on this together."

"Yeah!" Charlie sat cross-legged and looked up through the canopy. "Maybe Darren and Justice can come over when it's done."

"If you like."

The boy's enthusiasm faded, and he pointed over Heath's head. "We should probably tell my mom about that, though."

Heath dropped his head back and looked straight up. Seeing nothing but leaf clusters and blue skies, he twisted around to look at the other trees, wondering if he really needed to clear them out right now. Suddenly, molten terror streaked through his chest, and he scrambled away from the tree trunk on all fours then sat back up on unsteady haunches. In a nearby pine tree, a white-and-gray papier-mâché–looking wasp nest the size of a cantaloupe bustled with activity. Large, black-winged insects darted in and out. Heath's pulse thundered in his ears as he tried to collect himself. It was far enough away he hadn't noticed it, but if the wasps were ever disturbed or noticed him… He fought the urge to leap to the ground and run by telling himself he'd break his legs. Then, with a stab of guilt, he remembered the child beside him.

"Charlie," he whispered in a controlled voice. "I want you to get down right now, and do it quickly and quietly."

"Why?" From the corner of his eye, Heath felt the boy's stare, but he couldn't take his eyes off the wasp nest.

"Just do what I say. Right now. I'll be right behind you."

"Okay," said the boy tremulously. "But they're just wasps."

Heath realized he might frighten Charlie, so he forced himself to scoot across the platform and slide off silently before reaching for his little friend. Once the boy had a sneaker on a foothold, they broke their grip, and Heath slid the rest of the way down the trunk. Bark pulled on his shirt and scratched his midriff like fingernails. He skirted the stepladder and dropped to the ground, looking up to see if they'd disturbed anything.

Charlie broke the silence from beside him when he landed with a thud. "Wasps only sting if they're annoyed."

Heath took a deep breath, eyes on the nest. "They're very dangerous." He reached for the boy's hand and pulled him away from the beech tree.

"Anything's dangerous when it defends itself."

Heath tore his concentration from the wasps. "What?"

"Wasps don't bother you if you don't bother them," said Charlie with a touch of impatience.

"The tree house is too close to them, Charlie. Promise me you won't climb up there again." He gave the boy a penetrating stare until his little brown eyes dimmed.

"Yes, sir, Mr. Heath." The words oozed with disappointment. Heath ignored the fact he'd just promised to rebuild the tree house. He pointed toward the Harding property. "You better get back home before your mom gets worried."

Understanding this was not a suggestion, Charlie frowned. "Okay, but let me get my ladder."

Heath held up both hands to stop him. "I'll bring it over later. You head back now."

The boy grunted and stalked off toward home before stopping a few yards away. "Bye, Mr. Heath. I'll see you later when we fix up the tree house."

Heath gave him a pained smile. "Okay, Charlie. Later." He let the smile fall when Charlie turned away. He felt light-headed and damp, and his heart was racing like a speedboat. The child's father had promised him a fishing trip but passed away before he could make good on it. Now Heath had made another big promise, but he wasn't going to be able to follow through. His heart pinched. Poor Charlie.

Heath released a shaky breath. Remembering Trooper, he pursed his lips to whistle, then caught himself. Gulping, he started for the house on high alert, watching for any annoyed wasps that might be following him and hoped Charlie sent Trooper home if he saw him. Heath's throat was too dry to try to call the dog back.

Charlie talked relentlessly about the Underwoods' tree house while Ali tried to convince him to try some of her lip balm on his chapped lips before school. She realized she'd have to thank Heath for making the kind offer.

After dropping her son off, she made a beeline for the Gracious Earth. Pewter-gray clouds tumbled by, leaving raindrops on the windshield. She hopped out and dashed for the front door of the herb shop, unavoidably inhaling fragrances wafting over from the Last Re-Torte. The chimes on the shop door toggled when she burst inside, making Tam bolt upright from beneath the counter. Ali laughed. "It's just me. I'm sorry. The rain's here."

Tam's cheek quirked. "We need it, although I was going to stop by the Martins' you-pick after lunch to buy a quart of strawberries."

"They're in now?"

"Yes," said Tam. She stacked a pile of recycled paper bags onto the counter. "I don't have time to pick them myself. You should take Charlie."

Ali joined her at the register. "I don't think he'd enjoy picking strawberries, since he already complains about his gardening chores."

"He isn't wielding the bee smoker yet?" Tam grinned.

"I'm sure he'd love to try it, although I prefer a fume board."

"Maybe you could ask your neighbor to go strawberry picking with you," teased Tam. "Tell him the bees won't bother him because they prefer fruit." She reached for a reel of receipt paper and missed Ali's eye roll.

"I doubt he'd go anywhere bees are pollinating," said Ali. "He said he doesn't garden."

Tam snorted, pulled open the register and handed Ali a check. "This is last month's."

"Thanks." Ali exhaled with relief when she saw enough for groceries. The rest had to go toward May's loan payment, because she'd had to put April on her credit card after she'd paid the surveyor. It'd left little room for Charlie's birthday.

"Have you heard anything more about a fence?"

"You must be reading my mind." Ali waved the check. "No, Heath hasn't committed to putting another one up yet. He doesn't have to."

"Huh," said Tam. "You'd think since Trooper was stung he'd want something there."

"Exactly. That's what I thought, but I guess he doesn't have it in his budget for the cleanup. The man likes to keep his numbers in the black." Ali thought about Charlie's earlier excitement. "Yesterday, Charlie climbed up into a tree house on his property with him, and Heath promised him they could fix it up this summer."

"How nice." Tam leaned back onto the counter behind her. "Maybe you can help, too." She grinned mischievously. "Group project."

"I don't know," said Ali slowly. "He teaches classes online most of the day, then I guess he works on the house, which he has to finish along with the landscaping before this fall." She tapped the counter with the edge of the check. "Although this morning he did take the time to drop off a ladder Charlie left in the woods."

"Why not ask him if he meant it?"

"I guess I should. Charlie doesn't need any more disappointments right now. My credit card has a lot on it, which means there'll probably be no room for his birthday trip. I've got to find cash." The thought that Heath would take more time off from cleaning his parents' property to rebuild a tree house was touching, but what if it was just words? Keith had told Charlie every year since he was tiny they'd go deep-sea fishing the next year, then it'd been too late. Ali had promised herself she'd make her son's wishes come true no matter what it took, but the business wasn't growing as fast as she needed. "I overestimated how much honey I'd make last year and how much we'd need to live comfortably until this summer, and I didn't plan for Charlie's birthday at all."

"You've paid off medical bills, funeral expenses and a car, and you paid cash for that house when you moved here. The business is going to grow."

"I hope so," Ali said. "I just wish I'd thought about using the money for the business. This loan is hard to meet, but I guess a mortgage wouldn't have been any different." She sighed. "I can't help but wonder if I made a mistake moving to Lagrasse, Tam. I prayed about it long and hard, and I really felt it was the right decision."

"Look how everything fell into place." Tam came around the counter and gave her a hug. "You've only been operating for over a couple years. Don't panic." She searched Ali's eyes. "Be patient with the timing. You've started more hives, and you're on your way to doubling what you started with. You'll be in the black in no time."

"If things work out," admitted Ali. "Fighting to break even this spring has me doubting everything."

"But you got through it."

"Charlie's birthday is this month," Ali reminded her. "And that fishing excursion is so expensive. A day or two is all I'll be able to afford. I can't risk another credit card, and I'm terrified to ask for an extension."

"Where is your faith?" asked Tam point-blank. "You can't throw it all away at the first sight of every shadow that looms in the distance. You've already conquered a mountain most women will never have to climb."

Tears stung Ali's eyes, and she pulled Tam back in for another embrace. "You're right."

Tam returned to the other side of the counter as a bell jangled and a customer walked inside.

"You let me know, and I will find a way to help you out." She jabbed her finger in the air.

"No," resisted Ali. "I couldn't ask you to do that after all you've done for me."

"Do what?"

Ali turned around at the familiar voice. Angie Coles smiled back. She had an umbrella under one arm and a bag from the bakery under the other. It smelled like pastries.

"Nothing," said Ali quickly. "Tam is just being her usual helpful self." She zoned in on the paper bag. "I don't know what you have there, but it smells like it dropped from heaven."

Angie held up the Last Re-Torte sack like a trophy. "I am single-handedly keeping this business afloat." She opened the bag and let Ali have a peek inside. "It's a chocolate-raspberry torte."

Ali cast a woebegone look at Tam. "Thank goodness I'm broke right now, or I'd be funding the bakery, too, not to mention forced to work out every day."

Tam laughed. "It's called crowdfunding, ladies." They giggled, and Ali realized she needed to get back to the apiary to check on the new bees. She took her purse off the counter, tucked the check inside and gave Tam and Angie a wiggly-fingered wave. "I'll see y'all later. It's time to make the doughnuts." She laughed at her own joke and darted out to the car.

The sprinkles had become determined raindrops. After a quick stop to deposit the check at the bank, she cruised home in the rain, humming as the wipers swished water off the windshield. Soon they began to squeak, and a quick look overhead showed the storm had moved on, so Ali clicked the wipers off as she pulled into the driveway. When she climbed out, she searched the glistening atmosphere for a rainbow but was disappointed. An excited yelp made her freeze midstep.

"I know that bark," she said in a playful tone. She looked around for Heath, aware her heart had begun thrumming in anticipation of seeing him. Now would be a good time to ask him about the tree house. Trooper yelped again, and Ali strode to the backyard. He sounded close. And he was. In fact, Trooper leaped up on her shoulders, covering her in mud as soon as she latched the gate shut behind her. She put a hand on his head and gently pushed him away, then wiped off her hands. "What are you doing all the way over here, Trooper? You're going to get stung." She scanned the trees, wondering why Heath had let his dog get away, then she saw chunks of overturned soil all over the garden. The tidy rows of early spring vegetables and sprouted seedlings she'd transplanted from the greenhouse had disappeared beneath piles of capsized earth. Panic seized her.

A rabbit skittered out from under one of the blueberry bushes, making her jump, and it raced like a roadrunner for the side fence. Trooper yipped with joy and took off after it. Heart slamming into her breastbone, Ali lurched to the garden with a roiling stomach, gasping when she saw the full extent of the damage. Herbs were flattened, and cabbages and lettuces littered the wet yard like there'd been a wild party. The week's produce was ruined. No, she thought, as reality crashed into her, not the week's— the month's. Her entire spring garden was decimated, and she'd have nothing to sell at the farmers market but a few jars of honey. She put a hand to her chest to keep it from exploding. Trooper zigzagged back across the yard. Ali's hands shrank into tight fists.

"Trooper!" she shouted in her Mom-has-lost-it voice. "Come here!" The dog stopped and looked at her in surprise. Ali marched over and grabbed his collar. Somehow, she led him to the car without losing any more of her cool, but tears poured down her cheeks like the morning's rain.

The outdated doorbell echoed like a gong, and Heath frowned in the reflection of his computer screen. He'd started late because he'd noticed a wet spot on the ceiling in the kitchen and had to find a box fan to dry it out. That meant he'd have to paint over it later, but the leak would need to be located first. Playing with the numbers on his spreadsheet in order to work a new roof into the budget had shown he'd have to forget about cutting down trees for now. Tagging his spot on the screen with the cursor, he pushed back and plodded down the hall to the front door, noting the living room and kitchen were at least organized. It gave him a sense of satisfaction he hadn't felt in a long time.

The doorbell complained again, and, unable to see through the small bottle-glass window, he pulled it open to find a wet, shaggy and filthy Trooper. Ali had a firm grip on his collar, and her pretty freckled face was so magenta it made her hazel-green eyes glow like emeralds.

"Trooper!" he said in surprise. Ali tugged the dog forward, and Heath guided him into the house. "Get in here!" The dog scrambled off to the kitchen, flicking mud everywhere. "I'm sorry. I didn't know he got out."

Ali looked upset. More than upset. She looked like a smoking volcano about to blow. Heath cleared his throat. "I took the trash out just before it began to rain," he faltered. Her cold silence made him uncomfortable. Had Troop been in the hives again? "Are you okay?" She grimaced and shook her head. "What happened?" Heath asked with concern. Ali swiped at a lock of dark red hair on her forehead that reminded him of cinnamon. "Ali?"

Suddenly her hands went to her hips. "Trooper was in my backyard. Again."

Heath had visions of swarming bees. His stomach dropped like a rock. "He looks okay."

"Yes, he's okay, but my garden isn't." The words were as sharp as razors.

"Oh, no." Heath noticed the mud and clay on her jeans. He exhaled with dread. "How much damage?"

"Damage?" she repeated, her voice taut. "He *destroyed* it. Everything is trampled or dug up. It looks like there was a mud-wrestling match."

"I'm so sorry," said Heath, mortified. "That doesn't sound like him at all."

"There was a rabbit," Ali explained through gritted teeth. "I'm having more problems with them with the fence down, and I don't have the money to put another one up."

"Right." Heath frowned. "You're saving money for Charlie's birthday."

"It's more than that," Ali snapped, and to his horror, a tear welled up in the corner of her eye. "It's been tough making payments on my loan for the business since last winter, and the vegetables were my safety net." She sniffled. "I'm going to be short this month with nothing extra to sell at the market, then there's Charlie's birthday trip that I'd planned to put on a card I had to use in April. I don't want to have to ask the bank for an extension!"

"I'm truly sorry, Ali," said Heath glumly. He'd been so absorbed in his classes, and so satisfied to have the majority of the house cleaned up inside, he hadn't considered what she was dealing with on the other side of the pasture.

Forgetting Trooper's whereabouts was completely on him. "I'll pay for the loss," he said, quickly dismissing his spreadsheet's balance. "It was my fault after all."

"That's not why I came over," she said firmly. "I was bringing back your dog."

"I know that, and I appreciate you bringing him home," Heath replied. "But I insist."

"No." She shook her head stubbornly, and he wondered if it came with the red hair. "Not this time. All I ask is that you keep your dog inside or on a leash."

"With all this land?" Heath huffed. "You're right. I should have paid attention to where he was, but I'm not going to tie up my dog. That'd be like…" He hesitated and thought of Charlie. "You wouldn't keep Charlie locked up in the house or on a rope outside." Then he remembered the wasps in the pine tree. "In fact, I need you to keep Charlie on your side. He can't just wander around my property alone. It's dangerous."

Ali's jaw dropped, and her eyes narrowed. "You want me to keep my son off your land? Fine." She lifted her chin. "You keep your dog on your side, and I'll keep Charlie on mine." She pivoted on her heel before he could explain.

"Ali, wait."

"No, you're right," she tossed back over her shoulder as she strode down the sidewalk. "I think it's best. That way you can get your house cleaned and rented out, and I can stop worrying about your dog getting stung or dancing on my cabbages."

Heath followed her as she stalked to the car. "I'll check into a fence," he called, numbers and schedules wiggling to fit together in his head along with the new roof. He wondered if there even was a fence that could keep a dog and boy separated. He and Ali certainly didn't need one.

Chapter Eight

Ali drove the half mile back to her house, pulled into the driveway and slammed her door after climbing out of the car. She stumbled to the backyard to reexamine the damage, then grabbed a plastic bucket and a rake and headed for the first row of decimated vegetables to begin smoothing out the earth. Picking up the bits and pieces of her plants made her stomach heave with disappointment. She should have accepted Heath's offer to pay for the vegetables. Her foolish pride had gotten in the way. He'd let her pay for half of Trooper's vet bill after the bee stings. It would have only been fair, and to be honest, it would have helped.

She stopped and cupped her hands over the rake handle. The weather had climbed to a pleasant temperature, and she offered a prayer of gratitude that it wasn't late July. Would things be worked out by then? She prided herself on how well she'd managed as a single parent so far, but ever since Heath and Trooper had moved in, it seemed like the life she'd rebuilt was beginning to crumble. And all because of a stupid fence. With her credit cards almost maxed out, and Charlie's birthday, she might have to ask the lender for an extension this month after all. The thought filled her with dread, and she contemplated how to get around it.

Ali went back to raking the foamy clay dirt. Her throat tightened with a lump as big as an orange. Tears threatened, but she distracted herself by considering the progress of the buckets of tomatoes along the back porch. Thank goodness she'd decided to pot them this year. At least she'd have those on her market table soon. A bee flitted around her face, and she took a reflexive step back to give it room. In the distance, the colonies sang, blissfully unaware of how much she needed them. The second pair of new hives caught her eye, and she sucked in a determined breath. It was time to build the last set. She had a business to build, and that required more bees to make honey. It was thanks to Trooper and his owner that she was further behind.

More storms moved in and bellowed throughout the night, finally growing hoarse and quieting by morning. After a damp day at the farmers market where she sold little, Ali drove straight home to start melting beeswax for another test round of lip balm. The herb garden had not taken as much damage as the vegetables so she could use the rest of her dried mint and lavender knowing there was more outside for later.

Charlie sat at the table working on his science fair project. She was just beginning to feel less stressed when she heard a knock at the door. Praying for a pastry from the Last Re-Torte, she hurried to open it, thankful Tam had let her complain during a phone call that morning. She swung it open to find Heath on the porch steps covered in mud and looking like someone had tossed pepper in his eye. Her stomach dropped with disappointment when she realized there'd be no sugar rush. He had an enormous roll of chicken wire under his arm.

"Hi," he said as if he expected her to bite his head off.

Ali realized he'd taken the brunt of her frustration meant for rabbits and playful dogs. "Hi," she said, feeling ashamed. "I was hoping someone had come bearing pastries."

"Sorry." He smiled faintly. "I thought of something else."

"Chicken wire?"

"Yes. We have tons of it. I pulled it up from around the garden. You can have it."

"That was nice of you." Ali considered the

money she'd save. "I should have used it to start with. I just never got around to it."

"We're all busy," said Heath. "You're occupied with your son and the hives."

Ali heard Charlie rush up behind her. "Hi, Mr. Heath!"

Heath smiled at him, but Ali remembered his request to keep Charlie off his property. It made her feel bristly all over again, and she hesitated to invite him inside. He was muddy anyway… but he had brought her chicken wire.

"I can just set this at the corner of the house," Heath offered in the awkward pause, and she nodded.

"Thank you."

He swallowed. "Do you want me to set it up?"

"In the backyard?" she clarified. Was he offering to work in her garden with all he had to do at his place?

"Yes, if you need me to." White splotches appeared on his face. "I can stake the garden and wrap this around it if you want."

Ali thought of the hives humming in the distance and knew without asking he was terrified at the thought of them.

"That'd be fun. Can I help?" interrupted Charlie.

"No, you have homework." Ali motioned toward the kitchen with her chin. "Scoot, honey-bee."

Charlie moaned. "Fine. Okay." He poked his head under her arm and grinned at Heath. "I can help later, maybe."

Ali's nerves twitched. If Heath worked in her yard, it meant spending more time around him, and she didn't need the distraction any more than Charlie did. "No, it's fine. I'll do it. Thanks for the wire." Ali pointed toward the kitchen for Charlie's benefit, and the boy stomped away. Darting a look of amusement at Heath, she eased out onto the stoop beside him and closed the door. "Here. I'll take it." She held out her arms, but he only gave her one of the rolls before walking down the steps. Ali followed him. "I spoke to Charlie on the way home from school yesterday," she said conversationally.

"About what?"

Had he forgotten already? Heath had practically forbidden Charlie from setting foot on his land again. "About staying off your property."

"Oh, yeah," said Heath as they rounded the corner of the house. He set the roll of chicken wire down by the gate. Ali caught a drift of soap blended with a tangy and deep cologne. It reminded her of the woods in autumn and made her so tingly she tripped. He caught her by the elbow. "Got it?"

"Yes," she said, blushing at her clumsiness, or was it the touch of his hand? It felt like lightning, but at the same time, grounded her as if she were a live wire. How? Heath Underwood was just a comfortable and companionable guy, she insisted in her mind—until she met his gaze. Funny how such a bright shade of blue eyes could look so deep.

Attraction skittered through her veins, and she chuckled like something was funny. It *was* funny. They were on the verge of going at it like the Hatfields and McCoys, yet they could work more than well together when they had to do it.

"Okay," she sighed. She set down the chicken wire. "I need to apologize. I'm sorry. I didn't mean to be so rude when I brought Trooper back. I was really upset. I don't like to ask for help."

Heath's cheek tweaked as if he was suppressing a smile. "I gathered that."

"I guess I'm trying to prove I can do this by myself."

"Charlie," he said.

"Yes. Raise him on my own and run a business." Ali caught herself tapping her thumbs on her fingers. "I want my family to be proud, and his father, too. I don't want to have to go to work someplace else," she explained. "I quit a job at a garden center I'd managed for years after I had Charlie, but I had to go back after Keith died.

That meant other people were raising my boy. Charlie and the bees are all I have. Beekeeping always interested me, and Keith promised I could try it one day, but it never happened. His life insurance helped me buy a home here and get things in order, so I thought this was the right time."

Heath nodded as if he understood. "I wish you'd let me compensate you for the vegetables Trooper destroyed, especially since I took down the fence."

Ali reminded herself that humility paid more dividends than pride. "If you wouldn't think me too wishy-washy, I'd like to accept."

"Thank you." Heath exhaled with obvious relief.

"You're thanking me?"

"Yes. It makes me feel better about not putting up a fence right now."

"I get it," she admitted. "You're going to rent your house out anyway. It's not likely it will be to someone with a herd of border collies."

"Right, and the house is going to need a new roof, speaking of insurance. I just found out in last night's storm, although it didn't come as a shock."

"I'm sorry. Thank you for the compensation." Ali motioned toward the trees in the back, saddened she had to forbid her son from playing in the woods. "I'll make sure Charlie doesn't come over anymore."

"It's not that I don't enjoy his visits," Heath began, but he was cut off by the very subject, who appeared on the other side of the fence, having no doubt slipped out the back door.

"Hey, Mr. Heath," said Charlie, as if he hadn't just seen him.

Ali rolled her eyes. There was no keeping them apart. Her son was as infatuated with Heath as he was with Trooper. Not that she could entirely blame him—about the dog, she hurriedly added. "What happened to homework?" She raised an eyebrow.

Charlie rested his arms on the fence between them with a nonchalant air. "I had to ask Mr. Heath something."

"What's that?" said Heath, amusement highlighting his tone.

"Can you go to the science fair with me?" Charlie asked.

The man beside her hesitated, and Ali stiffened in surprise. When had Charlie decided to issue invitations without consulting her first? "Um, I'm sure Mr. Heath is busy next week," she stammered.

Charlie ignored her. "You like math *and* science. You said so. And it's a whole science fair."

"Wow."

Ali could tell by Heath's one-word reply that he was struggling for a polite answer. "It's on a Friday, honeybee," Ali reminded Charlie. "I'm sure Mr. Heath has tests and stuff."

"It's not during school," Charlie insisted. His eyes pinned Heath down so he couldn't escape. "It's at night so all the parents can go."

"I, uh," Heath began with a strange ripple in his tone.

Charlie raised his hands. "Sam Tuckey is building a rocket that uses chicken you-know-what for fuel."

A laugh shot out of Ali before she could stop it, but she slapped her hand over her mouth anyway. "Charlie!" she cried between her fingers.

"Really?" choked Heath. He seemed genuinely interested, and Ali realized how much her son wanted him to go. She saw Charlie's intense gaze and remembered he wouldn't have his dad at the fair, a fact she'd given no thought to, but apparently he had. She held her breath. If Heath didn't want Charlie on his land, he surely wouldn't want to go to his science fair. Perhaps it was best. They saw each other enough, and things were beginning to feel… Well, she was beginning to feel things, she admitted, and that wouldn't do.

"Umm…" murmured Heath. He looked at

Ali with a question in his eyes. "If your mother doesn't mind, I guess I could go."

"Yay!" Charlie cheered.

"I don't mind," admitted Ali, wondering why she felt relieved and why that made her cheeks toasty. "But you should know his project is about bees," she warned Heath. She waited for him to recoil. Instead, his face morphed through a range of emotions before settling on a polite but taut expression.

"That's okay," interjected Charlie. He beamed at Heath. "You don't have to see it if you don't want to. We can look at rockets."

Heath laughed. "I'm sure it'll be fine. I want to check out your work."

"Awesome! Can you help me with my homework now?"

"Charlie," scolded Ali in surprise. "I can help just fine. Now go back into the house." She gave him a menacing stare, and he scurried for the back door.

Heath folded his arms. "If you're sure you don't mind, I can drop by the fair."

"He'll like that, obviously. It's in the gym."

"Good." Heath scratched his forehead, then gave her an apologetic look. "I hope the chicken wire helps, and I'll have a long talk with Trooper."

Ali chuckled at the image of him scolding his dog the way she scolded Charlie. "Thank you."

"I'll get the money for the crops Trooper tore up to you by next Friday, then, if that's okay."

"Sure," said Ali with a smile of surrender. "That'd be great."

Heath hesitated as if trying to figure out how to leave, and she took a step back. There was no need to continue shaking. Contact with him was unsettling. His long fingers and tidy, even nails made her want to examine his hands more closely. She wondered if he had a perpetual ink stain on a fingertip like some teachers. He gave a friendly wave, and she watched him pull out of the driveway with tangled emotions. How strange that fences, bees and even naughty dogs weren't enough to keep them from going to the science fair together next Friday night.

With a helpless shake of her head, Ali walked slowly inside. Her mind whirled around lip balms, Charlie's homework and the work left to do in the garden. It would have been a lot easier to sort out if the man who lived behind her wasn't spinning around with them, too. She hoped she could keep a fence up around her heart until he got his house rented out and moved back to Alabama. It was surprising that she even needed one, she mused. She'd packed away all her dreams of having a partner for life when she'd become a widowed single mother.

Which meant the sooner Heath left, the better—before her son fell completely in love with him.

Heath fought a headache on Sunday and spent the morning going through old family albums and scanning pictures instead of attending church. He hadn't stopped thinking about Charlie's invitation to the science fair for days, but Ali was the real distraction. Determined to keep his attention on her son, he pulled into the elementary school on Friday evening ready to discuss rockets and brace himself for bees. Climbing out of the car, he smoothed down his pants, glad he'd had time to change after crawling onto the roof to paint a temporary seal over the source of the leak.

Children danced by, attached to their parents' hands, and he tried not to feel like a fish out of water. He would have had a child this age if things had worked out, but they hadn't. Exhaling, Heath headed for the front doors that looked the same as they had when he'd walked out of them for the last time in fifth grade. Once inside, he bobbed along in a streaming crowd through familiar halls that smelled of floor wax, lemon cleaner and cafeteria leftovers. By the time he reached the gymnasium, infectious excitement had permeated his reserve, and he found himself smiling at the packed room of tables and cardboard displays. A flash of auburn under the lights caught his attention, and he spotted Ali chatting with another woman next to a bright yellow cardboard trifold. Charlie stood in front of it wearing a wrinkled dress shirt with an adult-size tie knotted around his neck. "Mr. Heath!" Charlie screeched above the din. He waved like a madman.

Heath laughed at the boy's excitement and walked over, catching himself before he opened his arms for a hug. Instead, he gave Charlie's shoulder an affectionate squeeze. "Wow, Charlie! Look at all this."

The boy giggled, then pointed at his display. There were close-up pictures of bees glued to it, and Heath pretended he found them fascinating instead of disquieting. "So what's this about, exactly?"

Charlie picked up a teacher's pointer from his table and waved it with a flourish. He pointed at a graph. "My project is about what kind of nectar bees like best."

"Impressive." Heath felt Ali's examination and turned to greet her. She gave him a wink, and he bit the inside of his cheek to keep from grinning back.

"Bees need a balanced diet," explained Charlie. "They like herbs and flowers. I counted all the bees in our herb garden after school for thirty days. I also counted them on the flowers in Mom's flower bed."

"And what did they like best?"

"They liked the lavender best of all," Charlie declared. "I planted some plastic flowers, too, but they didn't like any of those."

"That's really interesting," said Heath. Charlie pointed his stick at a glass case on the table, and Heath craned his head politely. A bee's job was illustrated using actual specimens.

"See?" asked Charlie, motioning at a dried piece of lavender. "First they find a flower. Then they suck up nectar from it with their proboscis." He indicated Heath should look at a dead bee under a magnifying glass, but Heath kept his feet planted as if he could see it from where he stood. "Then, they go back to the hive and share it or spit it into honeycombs." The boy pointed at a tray from a hive. "The nectar becomes honey, and they feed their babies with it and store the rest to eat later." Charlie tapped a chunk of empty honeycomb and then a jar of golden honey.

"You sure know a lot about bees," Heath told the confident seven-year-old. Aware of Ali beside him, he dismissed a rising tide of memories so Charlie couldn't read his mind. It didn't work.

"They have four wings and compound eyes, and a stinger, too." Charlie pointed at a diagram of a bee's body on his trifold, then dropped to the next picture—an actual photograph of a bee's backside. "Do you know why bees sting, Mr. Heath?" Heath felt his smile tighten but shook his head. "Bees only sting in self-defense or to stop predators from stealing their honey," the child explained. "Sometimes they make mistakes. Mom said you got stung when you were my age," he admitted, and Heath tensed. Ali cleared her throat. "That was an accident, because you weren't trying to hurt them," continued Charlie. "They were swarming. Bees do that when their hive gets too crowded. That's how they grow another colony. They're looking for another place to stay, and if something scares them, they fight back." He gave a sorrowful wince, and Heath saw something desperate in his gaze.

Charlie really wanted him to like bees. Heath glanced at Ali, and she added, "They react to vibrations, pheromones and even certain colors."

Charlie turned back to his visual aids and pulled a honey stick from a bouquet in a clear vase. "Here. I brought you this. It's honey from our beehive. You said you eat blueberries, and our bees collect nectar from our blueberry bushes, so I think you'll like it."

Heath accepted the honey stick he'd refused at the farmers market. "Thank you." Charlie stared, and Heath felt Ali's gaze, too.

"Aren't you going to try it?" asked the little boy. "It has vitamins in it."

"Okay." Heath fumbled with the end of the honey stick until Ali handed him a pair of tiny fingernail clippers. He opened one end and put a dot on his tongue like a good sport. Charlie cried, "Wait! Here. Try it on a cracker."

Obediently, Heath smeared honey on a cracker sample and, through a mouth full of dry crumbs, said, "Mmm. Thank you." The sweetness was foreign to his tongue for only an instant before flavor watered his mouth. It didn't taste like blueberries, but it was familiar, and it brought a childhood memory forward in his mind. "I used to eat peanut butter and honey sandwiches with my grandfather when I was little."

Charlie beamed. "I love peanut butter and honey."

"Me, too," admitted Heath. "I guess I forgot."

"That's understandable," murmured Ali.

As Heath cleared the crumbs from his throat, he became aware of a gentleman standing on his other side. The man held a clipboard and wore a lanyard around his neck with a card inside it that read Judge. Heath took a step back and motioned him forward, but the judge smiled. "I already heard his presentation. You did a very good job, young man." Charlie looked like he might bust with pride. Ali took a few steps back to give him his moment, and Heath went with her as Charlie offered the judge a honey stick.

Heath licked his lips covertly and looked around the room. "He sure knows his stuff."

She gave a slight nod. "He's been so excited about this. He wanted to do an experiment baiting fish, but I had to explain to him I don't have the time to take him fishing."

"I'm sure he understands." Suddenly Heath wanted to offer to take the boy to the lake. "My dad has a fishing boat behind the tool shed."

"He wanted to catch a red snapper—and a marlin."

Heath chuckled. "Maybe some other time."

She glanced at him. "It's nice of you to offer."

"He did a good job on his project anyway. He's very independent."

"He doesn't have much choice." Ali looked around the room. "Everyone brought their families, but his grandparents live too far away to come for just a one-hour event, and he doesn't have any siblings." Her tone sagged.

Heath inclined his head with interest. "Did you hope to have more?"

"Yes." Ali's cheerful grin returned. "I'd hoped to have four or five children. It would have been a lot of fun, but it just wasn't meant to be."

Before even thinking about it, Heath said, "It's not too late."

She looked at him curiously, and he found a colorful trifold to study. "So, do you think you'll have children?" she asked.

"I hope so," murmured Heath. "Someday." His heart beat a little harder, ringing deeper in his soul than it had in a long time. Heath knew what he was missing, and it wasn't teaching on campus. It wasn't just his parents. He missed having a relationship. And yes, he genuinely wanted a child. A little girl or a boy. Like Charlie. He turned to Ali. "I know I'm no grandpa, but I hope you didn't mind me coming."

"I'm surprised you did, to be honest. Thanks for your support. It means the world to him."

"I'm sure it's not that big a deal."

"It is to Charlie. I know he bothers you a lot," Ali admitted. "You have so much to do before you head back to school."

He was busy, but Heath realized she thought he had more going on than he actually did, or maybe she thought he didn't enjoy Charlie's company. "I love having him around," he insisted. "My brother's children aren't nearby, and although Trooper has my heart, he doesn't do science fair projects."

Ali dropped her head back and laughed. The merry sound made Heath laugh, too, until the room around them quieted. A party of judges walked down the center aisle of the gym with a trophy and ribbons in their hands. Everyone cheered as first place was awarded to a student with a drone. Second place went to a little girl with a recycling experiment. Charlie sighed out loud with disappointment, and Heath resisted the urge to hurry over and comfort him. He crossed his fingers as the judges continued to spread across the aisles with the remaining award. The gentleman Charlie had engaged separated from the group and walked straight to the beekeeping project. Heath felt his throat constrict as Charlie's eyes widened. The judge taped a ribbon on his trifold board and handed him a medal. Ali sucked in a small gasp and put her fingers to her lips. Charlie's mouth quivered, and Heath watched him smile away tears. The boy grinned wider at Heath, and he gave him a nod of approval while he clutched the medal to his chest. Overhead, the loudspeaker announced, "Third place to Charlie Harding."

The gym erupted into more cheers. Struck with uncharacteristic shyness, Charlie ran into his mother's arms, and she held him for a moment. When more clapping erupted for the honorable mention, Charlie looked up at Ali, and the look of love that passed between them flooded Heath with an emotion that left him longing. Ali looked over. "Let's go celebrate," she said to Heath. "Will you come with us?"

"Of course I will." Heath didn't even have to think about it. He opened his arms, and Charlie ran over and threw his arms around Heath's waist. "Thank you, Mr. Heath."

"Why, Charlie? I didn't do anything. You won all by yourself."

"I mean, thank you for coming with us." He looked over his shoulder at his mom. "Can we go to Pizza Pies?" Then he looked back at Heath. "Do you like pizza?"

"I love pizza," Heath confessed.

"All the guys play the video games," Charlie said in an attempt at a rather grown-up voice.

"Do they?" Heath wondered.

"Yes. They're old-timey. I bet you'll be good at them."

Ali hooted. "It's time to polish up your arcade skills, neighbor."

Heath grinned. "I think I can handle it."

As they started for the parking lot with Charlie between them, Heath remembered to pay Ali back for the vegetables Trooper had destroyed. He hoped it'd cover her pizza night for Charlie. He also hoped he was doing the right thing. Charlie was becoming very attached, but he wasn't the boy's father. He wasn't even family. How would Charlie feel once the house was on the market to be rented and he returned to campus? Would the little boy cope with the changes okay?

Heath gave Ali and Charlie a wave as he slipped into the driver's side of his car to follow them. Once summer was over, he would no longer be across the pasture but back at his rented town house in Alabama with nobody but his dog. He hoped *he* could handle it. He really did.

Chapter Nine

The chef on the Pizza Pies sign was almost as welcome a sight as Heath walking into the school gym. One made Ali's stomach perk up, the other her heart. Charlie was out of the car and inside the restaurant by the time Ali grabbed her purse and locked the car. Shaking her head, she hopped up the steps to the porch of the eatery, dodged a group of loitering teenagers and walked inside the gray-blue building. Garlic and toasted-cheese smells welcomed her. The lighting was dim, but colorful glass chandeliers scattered it around the room, and bright LED screens televised a soccer game that caused occasional cheers to go up. She scanned the dining booths to the left and, not seeing the boys, craned her neck over the partition to where the arcade was set up. Old-school games like PAC-MAN and Centipede beeped over the hubbub of the crowd. Ali stepped up to the register, wondering if Heath liked his pizza plain or loaded.

She was just about to order half of each when she felt someone brush up beside her.

"Here, let me get that," Heath insisted as she scanned the menu.

"No, I don't mind."

"Please? I insist."

Ali shook her head stubbornly. "I can't let you do that. We invited you."

"Yes, but I want to reward Charlie for doing his best tonight. It's what teachers do."

"Buy pizza?" she joked. She considered her cash shortage despite the refund on the destroyed produce she'd just received, and softened. But Heath had done so much already. "He's so happy you came. Why don't we just split it?" suggested Ali.

"Okay," Heath relented, but she could tell he wasn't satisfied. It was heart-stirring that he wanted to buy their dinner. It wasn't even his special night.

"An extra-large," Ali told the cashier. "Pepperoni on one side and—" She looked at Heath. "Supreme on the other," he finished, lifting a brow for approval.

She grinned. "That's exactly what I was going to order." Ali handed him cash for half of the total and took three cups and a stack of napkins to the dining area to choose a table. She'd been wrong about him. So he didn't like bees. Or fences. He was more than cooperative and polite; he was a good man with a big heart. His devotion to Trooper suggested as much, but tending to his parents' estate and belongings on top of being so kind to a fatherless boy proved it. She wondered if he had a significant other at the university, then pushed away the thought. She'd had her time.

Heath arrived at the table she'd picked a few minutes later, and they chatted about life on campus until Charlie showed up out of breath. Wheezing, he put a hand on his chest. Before Ali could ask him if he needed more quarters, he huffed, "Mr. Heath, can you be on my foosball team? Darren just beat me two times in a row."

"Hey, I'm good at foosball, too," complained Ali.

Charlie glanced at her dismissively. "I know, Mom, but Darren's dad is playing."

Ali felt her cheeks warm, but there was reason to point out that Heath wasn't his father, not that he seemed to mind. As if sensing her apprehension, he gave her a wink from across the table. "If your mom doesn't mind calling us when the pizza gets here, I will."

"I promise." Ali hooked her thumb toward the arcade. "You two go ahead."

Heath slipped out of the booth and disappeared with Charlie. With a quiet sigh, she sipped her soda and surveyed the room until someone poked her shoulder. Tam grinned at her when she looked up.

"Girl, you scared me to death," chuckled Ali. "I'm glad you made it."

"Thanks for the text." Tam slipped down across from her on the other side of the table where Heath had sat. "It didn't take much to convince Piper to leave the house."

Ali laughed. "She'll be dating before you know it."

"No, she won't," grunted Tam. "I have enough to process just thinking about her in middle school next year." Ali flipped a coin in her hand and craned her neck to search the arcade for her ten-year-old goddaughter. "I already gave her change," said Tam. "I'm sure she'll find someone she knows."

"One of the benefits of a small town," Ali agreed.

"True. Most of the older kids are at the high school basketball game tonight."

"Or parties."

Tam groaned. "Don't remind me. Besides, your day will come. Charlie is right behind her."

"He's seven," pouted Ali. "He's going to be a little boy forever." She smiled at the wistful declaration, although she knew it wasn't true.

Tam scanned the restaurant. "So you said Heath was coming?"

"Yes, he's here." Ali tried to keep her expression neutral.

"Hmm," said Tam.

"Charlie invited him."

"Just like he invited him to the science fair?"

"That's right."

"And tomorrow he'll be at the farmers market."

Ali took a long draw of her soda. "What's your point?"

"Just that you two spend a lot of time together," said Tam.

"We're neighbors, and my child and his fur baby won't stay in their own yards."

Tam laughed. "Did he pay you for the loss of your spring veggies?"

"Yes, but I'm still going to be short, Tam." Ali sat back. "It makes me sick to my stomach. You know I want to avoid an extension, but this month's payment is going to be close even without Charlie's birthday trip crammed onto the credit card."

"Tell them the honey will be here soon. It's going to be okay."

Ali wanted to be brave. "I knew an unsecured loan would be a risk, but I thought I had the numbers all figured out. I never should have used my house as collateral."

"There are jobs in Lagrasse, you know."

Ali frowned. "I know. I just want to be there for my son every possible minute. Is that so wrong?"

"It's understandable." Tam reached across the table and squeezed Ali's hand while she fiddled with her straw wrapper. She almost choked on her emotions but somehow maintained her composure. She'd never wanted to be a widow. She'd never wanted a big career. All she'd ever wanted was to be a mother and have a home. Would anything she dreamed of come true? A steaming pizza appeared, and she welcomed the distraction.

"That pie looks delicious," Tam whimpered. "I better go make my order!" She jumped up and left. Ali thanked the server and arranged a few plates on the table as the pizza steamed into the air.

Remembering her promise to Heath, she got up and wandered across the restaurant. In the far corner of the arcade under glowing black lights, a furious game of foosball was underway with two teams of boys and men, and the adults were making as much of a ruckus as the children. With a flick of his wrist, Ali watched Heath sink a ping-pong ball through the other team's goalpost. He threw his arms into the air and began to whoop. Charlie shouted, "Yeah!" and they high-fived each other. Their competition groaned, but Darren's father offered to shake hands, and, laughing, Heath patted him on the back. The defeated team wandered off just as Charlie saw her and shouted, "Mom! We won!"

"Just by one point!" Darren called over his shoulder. Charlie stuck out his tongue at his tow-headed friend.

"Charlie," Ali warned, calling him back to earth. "Be a good sport."

"But, Mom, I never win." He looked at Heath with glowing excitement. "I've won two things today."

"That's right. The science fair and a foosball game." Heath laughed. His cheeks were ruddy, and a twinkle in his eye made him look so happy that Ali couldn't help but find him adorable.

"Your pizza is ready," she chuckled.

"Yay!" Charlie dashed off, and Ali turned to follow him.

Still catching his breath, Heath caught up beside her. "He's a fast learner."

"Is he?"

"Yes. Have you ever thought of putting him into sports?"

"That was never his dad's or my thing," said Ali. "I didn't think it was yours."

"Not exactly," said Heath. "I was into music and comics, but I love watching sports and keeping up with stats."

"That's right. I remember the Georgia Tech jacket from the closet."

They walked shoulder to shoulder back to the table. Tam gave Heath a wave from the register. He caught Ali's eye and smiled. "I forgot how friendly people are here in Lagrasse."

"It's a small town."

"A little smaller than Auburn," Heath allowed.

"You must be wondering if you'll ever make it back with so much left here to do."

Heath fell silent, but he took her hand and helped her slide into her side of the booth. At his touch, she found her gaze snapping to his, and in its depths she suspected she saw what she was feeling: an undeniable connection. She shifted her attention back to the table and ignored it. Charlie was already sliding a giant slice of pizza onto his plate, so Ali busied herself by helping him and pretending to laugh at the stretchy cheese. She tried to concentrate on dinner instead of Heath's flitting glances and wondered what was happening between them and why. It was beginning to take effort to push away the emotions he sparked inside of her whenever he was around. She stared at her pizza, almost slumping with relief when Tam and Piper joined them.

Piper ignored a challenge to play foosball from Charlie, but after listening to him boast, she changed her mind, and the two soon darted off after eating. It was a great night out with friends. *Friends*, Ali reminded herself firmly. The man across from her could not tolerate the sight of a bee, for goodness' sake, and she'd just settled into a routine and accepted her destiny as a single mom. There was no way she could fall in love with someone again. She didn't have it in her. Not now. Not Heath. She had a child and a business to nurture and grow. She didn't need anything else. It was ridiculous to even consider it, or him. Besides, Heath wanted his own family. He'd never expressed any interest in a starter set.

Heath awoke to Trooper rustling around the bedroom like a personal valet. The curtains over the window suggest dawn was just a few blinks away, but Heath's mind returned to the night before and dreams that had troubled him. Eventually, he dragged himself out of bed. Trooper was happy to be let out, and he kept a close eye on him, sipping a tall glass of orange juice at the kitchen's sliding glass door. It was more sugar than he needed, but it revived him.

The pizza had not set well. His troubled sleep couldn't be from spending time with Ali. It was just a science fair. He'd gone for Charlie's sake. But there was something about eating, talking, joking and laughing with Charlie, his mom and their friends that had made Heath feel like he belonged in Lagrasse, as if the old town had been waiting for him to come home. Then there was Ali herself. The outline of a freckled cheekbone when she turned her head. The way light and shadow made her auburn hair look magenta. And those lively eyes he wanted to walk through.

Heath exhaled in frustration and leaned against the door frame. Why was he thinking about his bee-obsessed neighbor in such a way? He was just home temporarily.

He watched Trooper sniff for any nocturnal critters who may have wandered through the yard overnight, wondering how the dog would behave once they returned to the town house in Auburn. There was no acreage around it like the house here in Lagrasse. Heath studied the trees that camouflaged the Harding property in the distance. There would be no Charlie at the town house, either. The thought made him sad, and he stepped out onto the patio and dropped into a damp lawn chair to watch the morning mist dissipate. The air smelled like honeysuckle and wet grass. It seemed to nourish his lungs with every breath, promising summer was on the way.

For a fleeting moment, he wished he was on the banks of the lake listening to the peaceful water lap up on shore with his dad. He smiled sadly to himself. No wonder Charlie couldn't wait for his fishing trip. It was too bad the boy didn't have his father with him anymore. Heath had at least had his dad throughout most of his life.

When Trooper was ready to be fed, Heath followed him into the house and afterward got dressed to head to the farmers market. He chose a box with some of his mother's porcelain clowns and the last of his father's baseball card collection. They were painful to part with, but neither he nor his brother had any desire to keep them, and they would make someone else happy. He loaded the collectibles up with Trooper and arrived at the market five minutes after the gates opened. He was looking forward to seeing Monk and spending a few hours with someone who shared his love of mathematics and had memories of his parents, too. Deeper inside, Heath knew he also looked forward to seeing Ali and Charlie again, although they'd just been together a few hours ago.

By ten in the morning, the market was bustling, and Heath swapped shifts with Monk every twenty minutes at the table to give his elderly friend's knees a break. Heath tried not to be obvious watching the other end of the shelter, where Tam and Piper had set up the booth for the herb shop, but by the time he could smell popcorn wafting on the breeze, he became concerned. Ali and Charlie hadn't arrived. "I should call Ali," he said to Monk, who was sprawled out in a camp chair with his hands cupped over his belly. He wore a black Vietnam veterans' hat over his thick hair and looked content.

"What for?" Monk raised a scraggly eyebrow.

"She's not here yet, and I know Charlie was looking forward to today."

Monk snorted. "That's because Charlie spends the whole time eating every dime she makes." Heath chuckled and leaned against the table. After he explained Trooper's annihilation of the Hardings' garden, Monk shook his head. "She's going to have to get more hives or come up with something else pretty fast."

Heath groaned, and Monk grinned. "I did try a honey stick at the science fair," Heath admitted. "Charlie taught me a few things about bees I didn't know."

"Good." Monk nodded at him. "That's how you get over your fear of something, Heath. You learn about it and then you confront it again."

"Uh, no, thanks," Heath replied. "I'm just getting used to the idea of having an apiary nearby, but I still wince every time I hear something buzz."

"That's only natural," said Monk. He motioned at the infantry crest on his cap. "I still flinch at loud sounds, and it's been over fifty years." Heath offered an empathetic smile.

"Hey, Mr. Heath!" Charlie's excited voice interrupted their conversation. Heath turned in happy surprise that was mingled with relief.

"Good morning, Charlie! How are you today?"

"Good." The boy grinned.

"I was getting a little worried about you. You guys are late."

Charlie looked over his shoulder. "Mom had work to do this morning. Guess what?"

"What?"

"She got some honey out, and I helped her."

Heath thought of bees swarming beekeepers while they robbed them of their honey and swallowed. "Did you?"

"Yes. It wasn't a lot, but we filled up four jars. I got to hold a smoker."

"That's nice," mumbled Heath. What on earth was Ali thinking, letting Charlie rob hives? Was she harvesting already? Would it be a monthly thing? Weekly? "Where is your mom?"

"Over there." Charlie pointed across the shelter, and Heath caught a glimpse of red hair that made his heart leap over his hurdles of nerves. He braced himself. After all she'd been through, how could she put her son in danger? What if disturbing her hives made the bees swarm? What if the bees chose his house to build a new home?

"I'll be right back," Heath said to Monk in a terse tone. He strode across the shelter, burning with apprehension. Ali looked up as he approached the table.

"Hi, Heath." Her smile was soft, and something in her eyes looked like she was happy to see him. Heath took a deep breath to calm the uncertainties. He realized he'd gone straight into both fight *and* flight at the same time.

"Good morning," he grumbled, struggling to compose himself.

"Hey, Heath!" Tam gave him a wave, and he offered her a tight smile. He watched Ali stack small jars of honey into a neat pyramid.

"Those are new."

"Yes," said Ali. "Since I'm running low, I thought I'd sell in smaller containers."

Heath segued right into her admission. "Charlie said you smoked your beehives this morning."

"Yes, just hive number seven. We got about two quarts."

Heath pursed his lips as if she'd given a confession.

"What?" she asked, amusement flickering in her eyes.

"You could have warned me," he said flatly.

"Told you what?"

"That you were opening a hive and stirring them up. You know they make me uneasy."

"I wasn't 'stirring them up,'" she replied, going on the defense. "I do the opposite. I keep them calm. You have nothing to worry about."

"But you let Charlie help."

"Yes. He's a great assistant, and he wants to learn. We just got the colonies established in twenty-nine and thirty."

She sounded offended now, but Heath couldn't stop. He had to protect Charlie and Trooper, and, he thought desperately, himself. "You shouldn't have let Charlie do that," he blurted. "He could have gotten stung several times."

"I know how to handle my bees, Heath," Ali countered. Behind her, Tam's eyes rounded in warning at Heath.

He ignored her and took a deep breath. "He's a child. It could kill him. They almost killed me."

Ali retorted, "I know how to take care of my son. Do you really think I'd ever do anything that might take him from me?" Tornadic clouds brewed in her eyes, and Heath knew he'd crossed a line. He hadn't meant to, but he'd been so worried.

"We wore protective gear, which I would have told you about if you'd asked," Ali finished. She stalked out of earshot. Heath exhaled in frustration. He glanced at Tam, and she gave him a surly look.

"I'm just concerned about what could have happened," he said helplessly to Tam. "I've never seen anyone harvest honey."

"Why didn't you just say that to start with?" Tam gave her head a toss and looked away.

Heath shuffled his feet, waiting for Ali to return, but she busied herself with boxes several feet away and appeared in no hurry. Tam caught Heath's attention again. "She's trying to come up with this month's loan payment to avoid asking for an extension and give Charlie the birthday present his father promised him. She can't take out any more credit."

Frustrated, Heath slunk back to his baseball cards and clowns. Guilt nibbled at him. He should have paid for all the pizza the night before. She would have fought him, but he could have found a way. For all her cheerful appearances, Ali was struggling, and Charlie was looking forward to this birthday trip. Of course she would start collecting what product she could for the farmers market, especially in a tight month that his dog had everything to do with. If he'd just left the fence in place, maybe Trooper wouldn't have dug up the garden, and Ali wouldn't have had to rob a hive so early to take care of her son. Heath shut his eyes, then opened them to find Charlie standing in front of him with a grin. He pointed at the table behind Heath. "Are those clowns?"

"They belonged to my mother."

"You aren't keeping them?"

"They give me the creeps."

"I think they're funny. Somebody will like them," Charlie predicted.

Heath watched him run a finger over one of the statues. He couldn't put the fence back up, but he could stop thinking about Ali as more than a neighbor. It was a boundary they both needed. And Charlie? Well, he couldn't take someone else's son deep-sea fishing, but Heath had something he suspected would be almost as good.

"Mom!" Charlie sounded like he'd just won the science fair all over again. Ali pushed a roll of cash into her pocket and looked up. He was glowing like he had the night before as he held up a model ship.

"What do you have?" she asked in concern. She looked around at the nearby vendors, then realized the ship looked familiar. "Where'd you get that, honeybee?"

"Mr. Heath gave it to me. Isn't it awesome?"

"He did?" Gratitude fluttered through her, but Ali shoved it back. "Why?" she asked suspiciously. "Charlie, you didn't ask him for it, did you? You're supposed to be saving your money."

"No, Mom," her son sang as if she were silly. "He just gave it to me because he trusts me to take care of it. He said it's for winning the science fair."

"That's very nice," Ali relented. She gave Tam the side-eye.

"He's quick to apologize," Tam pointed out. Oblivious, Charlie danced around them with the ship clutched in his hands.

"That's an apology?" Ali muttered. "He has my son wrapped around his finger."

"Not on purpose," argued Tam.

Ali exhaled in surrender. "I guess it was nice."

"He's sorry he made you upset," Tam insisted. "I think he panicked."

Ali stared into space as a woman approached the table, then wandered away. "He accused me of endangering my son."

"He just cares about him."

"I think he's more worried about bees." She stopped and tried to put herself in his shoes. "He still doesn't understand why they swarm, and he shouldn't have been so reactive. It's like he's a…" She grasped for the right word.

"A frightened little boy?"

"Yes. Thank you, Tam. It's true." Ali collapsed into a camping chair and crossed her arms, knowing she looked like a stubborn child. "The sooner he gets that property rented out and heads back to Alabama, the easier things will be on everybody." She tapped her thumbs on her fingertips. "I won't have to worry about any more fences being taken down. There won't be dogs in my garden, and…" She hesitated.

"You won't like him so much?" Tam suggested unhelpfully.

"No, I won't have to listen to complaints about my hives," Ali blustered. "Have you noticed that Charlie acts like he wants to be around him more than me?"

"Are you jealous?" teased Tam.

"No, I'm…" She looked up at Tam, perplexed. "I don't want Charlie to be depressed when Heath leaves, that's all. He already misses his dad. And then there's the fact that Heath over-reacts about his safety like I don't know how to take care of him. It's insulting."

Tam gave an understanding nod, then her eyes narrowed. "How old was Heath when he got stung?"

Ali thought back until it dawned on her. She looked at Tam grimly. "He was eight."

Chapter Ten

～

Potluck Sunday started bright and clear, but towering white clouds hinted that thundershowers were on the way when Heath pulled into the church parking lot. He'd felt uneasy the rest of the afternoon at the market the day before, even when Charlie scampered over and told him goodbye after lunchtime. Ali had stayed out of sight, but he'd seen her pacing at one point and noticed her side of the booth was empty. She'd sold all her honey, and he felt instant happiness for her, but he knew it was not enough. She had problems just like he did.

He'd tried watching a movie with Trooper, but the house felt too still, so he'd trudged into the office to grade assignments that'd been turned in early. At least he had his students—his work was what he'd thrived on for so long—but since coming back to Lagrasse and the memories that made up the building blocks of his cells, he'd felt...whole. Not like a fraction or a percentage. Just complete. It didn't add up.

He slunk into the sanctuary and listened to the sermon, keeping his line of sight straight ahead although every instinct inside him was aware of the bobbing garnet hair on the other side of the room. He chided himself again for opening his mouth and insulting Ali at the market. It wasn't his place. He wasn't a father, and their family business wasn't his problem. After the last *amen*, he gave Angie Coles a polite nod, shook hands with the pastor, then let himself out, refusing to admit that his heart hoped Charlie would say hello, but Ali had a firm hand on his elbow, clearly unwilling to let him out of her sight.

With a frown, Heath hurried back to his car, scooting the tortoiseshell glasses up on the bridge of his nose. He didn't really need them away from the computer, and he silently mocked himself for wearing the pressed slacks, blue oxford dress shirt and tweed blazer. He was dressed every bit like a professor. But so what? That's who he was. Wasn't he completely caught up on grading assignments? He'd even recorded his lesson videos through Wednesday.

By the time he pulled into his driveway, Heath found himself fighting emotional fatigue. The inside of the house was finished, but the outside was still derelict. The trash and random junk had been removed, but more than half of the flower beds and shrubbery were still painfully overgrown. The carport had paint peeling in places like an onion. Ignoring it all, he threw himself into grading assignments until he was able to take a phone call from his brother.

Monday arrived as a warm day with cool breezes. Heath sat in the car after a trip to the dump and stared at the house rebelliously. The work would wait forever if he let it. With a determined inhale, he climbed out of the car and trudged into the house. Trooper stretched and offered a welcoming bark, and Heath made them both a bologna sandwich, then changed into old clothes. In the storage room under the carport, he pulled out a bucket of paint he'd bought at the home store. It was a close match to the original color of the house's trim—a soft ocher that would look nice against the yellow-cream bricks. He backed his car out, swept off the concrete with a broom and dusted away cobwebs and old mud dauber nests. Chunks of hardened red clay left dust everywhere, so he swept the ground again, then pried open the paint can and gave the contents a stir.

Tires crunched in the driveway, and Heath looked up in surprise. His chest convulsed when he saw Ali's car. He arranged a polite smile on his face, wondering with apprehension what was on her mind this time. She certainly wasn't one to keep feelings to herself. He never had to worry about or analyze what she was thinking, which was kind of a relief. Charlie, ever the icebreaker, hurried straight to the carport with Trooper barking joyfully to get his attention. It worked. Charlie stopped, and the dog climbed all over him with licks and happy groans. Ali proceeded straight to Heath.

"We missed you at the potluck yesterday," she announced, as if Saturday had never happened. Her eyes darted to the open door of the storage room, and Heath realized she was holding a covered paper plate. She held it out. "Truce?" The smell of pulled pork hit his nose, and Heath's hand darted out to catch it without a second thought. "Thanks," he said. "I just ate, but I'd be happy to take it off your hands for later."

She smiled. "Charlie insisted we bring you something, and I had to agree." She looked around the carport. "Are you doing okay? I thought maybe you didn't feel well."

Heath motioned at the paint can. "I thought I'd get started out here, even though it's getting late."

"I'm happy to help," Ali offered.

"Me, too!" Charlie joined them and eyed the paintbrush on the ground.

"Let me take this inside, and you're both welcome to help if you don't mind getting dirty."

Ali waved him off. "You go ahead, and we'll

get started. I was going to offer to help you inside, but it sounds like you have most of that done."

"Yes, pretty much." Heath rushed the plate of barbecue inside and stowed it in the fridge, his day brighter and mood lighter. For the next two hours, he and Ali chatted while painting the inside of the carport and the iron scrollwork that served as a post for the corner of the house. By the time they finished the first coat, Charlie was splotched with brown spots like a dairy cow, and Ali was as freckled as ever. She looked adorable, Heath thought, as he surveyed their work. "I would have never finished this fast. Thank you, guys."

"We're happy to help."

"Yes, that was fun," said Charlie. "What's next?" Heath didn't point out that his mother had had to follow behind him cleaning up drips, but distant thunder interrupted their conversation.

"Uh-oh. I think that's enough for today." Heath felt a sudden chill as the temperature dropped. More spring rain was on the way. It was too late for lunch, but still a little early for dinner. "Why don't you two come inside and have something to drink? I bought a small cake at the market on Saturday. It's red velvet."

"I love cake!" Charlie cried. He skipped inside with Trooper at his heels. The dog was spattered with new spots, too. Heath grinned at Ali, and she shrugged helplessly.

"He just had cake at church yesterday."

"I'm sorry. How about Popsicles?"

She gave him a lopsided grin. "If you can talk him into it. The boy loves a sugar fix."

"I'll give it my best shot." They washed up in a sink in the storage closet, then found Charlie wrestling with Trooper in the family room.

"I put your ship beside our television and my dad's picture," he said when Heath returned from the kitchen with a soda and two bottles of water.

"How do you like it?"

"It's cool. I think I'm going to write a report on it next year. I'm almost in third grade," he reminded him.

"I guess that means school is almost out." Heath shot Ali a grin.

"Yes, and that means it's almost my birthday." Charlie balanced the soda on his knee and popped the top.

"Don't spill that," his mother warned.

"I'm not. I'll be careful."

"He's always careful," Heath agreed.

Charlie took a gulp then sighed. "I am, Mr. Heath. Right?"

"I know you try," Heath allowed. He turned to Ali. "I'm sorry about Saturday. It wasn't my place."

"You were just concerned about him. I should be grateful you care."

"I panicked a little," Heath admitted. "I was thinking..." He hesitated. Monk had reminded him that facing fear was the only way to conquer it. He couldn't hide in his spreadsheets forever, afraid to get stung. That wasn't living.

"Yes?" Ali was waiting patiently.

"Maybe I should come watch you one day." Heath's insides flinched, but he realized he'd rather face bees than what could happen between them.

"Watch me what?" she wondered.

"You know. Smoke the bees or whatever you call it."

Ali brightened. "I think that'd be a good idea. It'd be good for you."

Heath's palms dampened, and he wondered why he'd opened his mouth. But he knew. He was trying to reach her, to connect and to face the fear that had consumed him since childhood. He wanted to support Ali and to see her and her son happy before he went back to school. Her warm eyes found his, and he could have sworn electricity crackled through the air. It had to be the weather, he told himself.

"So, when is your birthday?" Heath blurted to Charlie, desperate to sidetrack his useless feelings.

"On May 25," chirped Charlie. He punctuated his sentence with a long belch, and Ali gasped,

"Charlie!" but the hilarity of the situation got the best of Heath.

"My brother could put you to shame," he hooted.

"I bet he couldn't," Charlie retorted. He took another swig of his soda.

In a firm tone, Ali said, "Charlie, please control yourself, or I'll have to reconsider your birthday trip."

The boy stopped drinking with a frown, then swallowed what looked like a painful bubble of air. Heath chuckled. "You don't want to miss out on your deep-sea fishing trip, do you?"

"No," Charlie hiccupped. "Can you go with us?"

The casual question caught Heath off guard. Saturday he'd crossed a line. Charlie wasn't his son—Ali had made that clear—and just this morning, he'd decided to stop listening to the suggestion echoing between his ears that he might be falling for a beekeeper. It was ludicrous and impossible. He had his life. They had theirs. Neighbors did not fall in love, especially ones with histories that didn't meet in the middle. The math didn't work.

Heath didn't like to think about caring so much for this little boy then never seeing him again. He couldn't bear to think of having someone like Ali and losing her. He shook his head brusquely. "Like I told you before, I get queasy, and I need to get ready for the fall semester. This trip is for you and your mom."

"He's right, Charlie," Ali agreed quickly. "This is our family trip, and Mr. Heath has to finish getting his house ready to rent." Heath tried to cover the jolt of pain she caused by excluding him as family, but it was true. He told himself he was relieved that she agreed.

Charlie frowned. "We can help him after the trip. He helps us."

Ali cleared her throat. "He was paying us back for Trooper's rabbit hunt in the garden."

"But he came to my science fair."

"Because you invited me, and I wanted to come," Heath inserted. "You two go just like your father promised and have a great time."

"I know my dad is watching over me, but I want you to come, too," Charlie pouted.

"Charlie," Ali began.

"No," the boy snapped. "Moms are dumb." He stalked out of the room, leaving Ali speechless. Her face reddened to a profound shade of scarlet, and Heath's heart almost cracked when he saw her eyes glisten with tears. The front door slammed shut.

"I'll go get him," Heath offered, educator instincts kicking in. Although he felt like he'd just surrendered something precious, he rose to his feet. "That was not okay."

"No." Ali swiped at her eyes. "I can take care of it."

"I know you can, but you don't have to all the time," Heath countered.

She gaped at him, eyes wide and fists squeezed shut. "Actually, I do. I'm the mom. There's nobody else, so that means it's all on me. I accepted it the day I said goodbye to his father. God has put this burden on my shoulders to carry."

Heath crossed the room before he knew what he was doing but stopped short of taking her in his arms. He reached for her hands instead. "I know what it's like to feel like you're on your own. You're doing amazingly well, but whatever you're trying to prove isn't necessary. One plus nothing doesn't equal two, Ali. Charlie needs you, but he's going to need other people in his life as well."

Ali's jaw tightened at the truth. He recognized it in her eyes as her shoulders slumped. When she raised her gaze to him, he saw shadows in their depths. Her voice sounded fractured. "If you're talking about a father, yes, I know he needs one, and I'm sorry he's attached himself to you." Before Heath could interrupt, she said in a rush, "I'm never going to go through that again—losing someone in such a horrible way. I don't want Charlie to go through it, either." She steeled her spine. "I won't be left twice, Heath, so if you're talking about me finding someone else, I mean, forget it."

There. It was out now. He knew. A rising tide of hope resolved itself in Heath's curious heart by slamming back down to his toes. Ali tore her gaze from his and studied the carpeting at their feet. "That's why I've got to make this fishing trip work. He has a father, and I need to keep his memory alive. That's all I can do."

Heath forced himself to breathe in and out to stop heat from flooding his cheeks. She didn't know he'd been struggling with feelings. Now he saw them for what they were and hated himself for allowing them to happen. He braced himself. No more walks to her backyard or school fairs. No more Pizza Pies. Moments like those made him think he was falling in love. It was nothing more than a silly, baseless calculation. "I understand completely," he said in what he hoped was a soothing tone. "I'm not ready to risk romance again, either." He shook his head in denial. "That betrayal was nothing like I'd ever felt before. My parents were so happy in their marriage, I naively thought I could have the same thing and jumped too fast."

"It doesn't mean you can't," Ali said in a whisper. Remembering her son, she glanced out the window where the skies had darkened, but Heath wondered if it was to break eye contact because their connection felt so intimate. He regretted he couldn't embrace her, if not for comfort. He wanted to feel her heartbeat.

He dropped her hands and stepped away. "I can't right now anyway," he mumbled. "I was born to teach, and that's something I do best alone." He forced himself to smile in order to hide the dismay churning in his stomach.

"I understand. I better go rein in my child." Ali gave him a nod and walked out of the room with an unsettled Trooper at her heels.

"Ali," Heath called after her. She looked back, and he saw she was fighting tears. "He didn't mean it," he said. "Charlie loves you."

"Sometimes I wonder," she grumbled as she reached for the door handle.

"Hey, I was a boy once, too," Heath reminded her. "We say dumb stuff."

Ali bobbed her chin, but no amusement softened her lips. Trooper whimpered when she nudged him aside and slipped out the door. Heath exhaled to relieve the tension in his body. Sometimes children could be cruel. His students were grown adults, and even they occasionally said things that hurt his feelings. He stared wistfully out the window, observing a heated exchange on the overgrown lawn that ended with Ali jabbing her finger toward the car, and Charlie stomping to the driveway. Tears streamed from his eyes. He looked toward the house, and Heath took a step back into the shadows. Poor Charlie. Heath was just as crushed. He actually wanted to go on the birthday trip, but that would just complicate things. Ali had drawn a clear boundary between them that his yearning feelings would have to respect. He was glad. They wouldn't have worked anyway.

Charlie was unreasonable the rest of the evening, and Ali put him to bed early so she could call Tam and complain. The next morning, her to-do list tumbled in her head like a clothes dryer as she sipped herbal tea over her Bible. The new bee colonies seemed to be thriving, but she needed to check the one she'd just robbed. Then there was the garden. In her little greenhouse, a third round of beans and squash seedlings was ready to go into the ground. They'd replace the plants Trooper had ruined. Ali wrenched her lips at the thought of the mischievous dog. She'd surrounded the garden in chicken wire, regretting she hadn't done it sooner. She still had a lot to learn, but at least the blueberries looked wonderful. She set down her teacup, noticing that Old Ironsides glowed in a sunbeam on the television stand. Charlie treasured the unsinkable ship as much as the man who'd given it to him. Her heart squeezed.

Heath's confession that another woman's betrayal had ruined him for good had hit her hard. She wondered why she'd felt the need to inform him she'd never marry again. She didn't know if it was true, but he didn't need to know the depths of the pit she'd been dropped into when she'd lost the love of her life. Everyone said she was so strong, but Ali knew she was killing herself trying to prove it. Heath seemed to sense that, and her attraction to him, but he'd made it clear he wasn't interested in taking any chances with his heart after a divorce. Apparently he'd make allowances for Charlie, and she appreciated that, but he sure had peculiar boundaries. She just didn't know if it was the bees or herself. Ali smiled at his quirks and wondered, if she hadn't owned bees, would he feel differently about her. An ache pierced her bones, and she let out a weighted breath she'd been holding.

"Charlie!" Ali broke the silence in the house with regret. She closed the Bible where she'd stopped to ponder the sixth chapter in Matthew, feeling a little more connected to a greater power she knew she had to trust if she was going to endure life faithfully. *For your Father knoweth what things ye have need of, before ye ask him.*

Ali climbed up, bracing herself for the new day with restored hope.

On the way to school with her still-surly son buckled in the back seat, she interrupted his window-gazing, hoping to resolve what troubled him. "I talked to Heath a few minutes yesterday after you hurt my feelings." Silence. "He really cares about you even if he isn't going with us on your birthday trip."

"If he liked me, he'd go fishing with me."

"This isn't like going to a science fair, honeybee," Ali explained. "Deep-sea fishing costs a lot of money, and it'll take half a day just to drive down there."

"So?"

"So, Mr. Heath has to finish getting his property done."

"Why doesn't he just live here?"

"Because he works at a university, remember?" Charlie made a disgruntled noise. "He probably would get seasick. Do you want to spend your whole birthday trip with someone barfing over the side of the boat?"

Charlie met her gaze in the rearview mirror. "Gross, Mom. He never said that."

Ali chuckled. The ice had finally broken. She suppressed the concern that she might have that exact problem if the seas happened to be rough.

"When do we leave?"

"Two more weeks," she said. "The day after you get out of school. I promise we'll go see Mr. Heath when we get back and tell him all about it."

"Can we buy him a souvenir?" asked Charlie hopefully.

"Sure." Ali cringed at another expense. Hopefully, Heath liked fish. She'd had to squeeze the reservation onto the credit card after all, which she'd hated to do, even with Heath covering Trooper's damage.

By the time she dropped him off in front of the school, Charlie looked content. He shouted, "Bye, Mom!" when he closed the car door and dashed inside. Her heart stung a little. He was getting older, more independent. It seemed like only yesterday she'd driven him to pre-K in the mornings and his dad had picked him up in the afternoons. She eased out of the school drop-off zone and headed for the Gracious Earth, her stomach complaining although it was too early for lunch. She squashed the inner temptation to stop at the Last Re-Torte. She needed every penny to avoid begging the bank for a pass this month. Inside, she found Tam at the counter. "Good morning," she called.

Tam looked up from over a ledger. "Happy Tuesday. Were you able to get Charlie to calm down?"

"Just now." Ali exhaled. "I promised him we'd visit Heath after the trip and bring him a souvenir."

Tam laughed. "I'm sure that's just what he wants."

Ali gave her a frustrated stare. "I told you it's nothing."

"Nothing? You two were finishing each other's sentences and laughing at everything the other said the entire meal Friday night. Saturday I thought fireworks would go off."

"He apologized, and we're just friends." Ali brushed her off, ignoring the fluttering in her heart. She wanted to catch it like a butterfly but couldn't risk being wrong and getting stung.

"Tell that to Charlie."

"He just misses his dad."

"Or knows something you don't."

"He's a child," Ali dismissed. "I told you Heath made it clear he doesn't want to marry again, either, and I totally understand that."

Tam frowned. "I wish he wouldn't encourage you."

"Why not? We get each other." Ali leaned on the counter eyeing the essential oil collection on the wall behind Tam. They were nature's potions grown by God that could ease the emotions and heal wounds one tiny drop at a time.

"You understand you've both been hurt," Tam

argued. "He obviously craves a family, especially with his parents gone. Cleaning out the house where he grew up happily is probably stirring up things he doesn't want to deal with because he had a bad experience."

Ali considered that. "I came to Lagrasse to move forward. Maybe he just needs to hurry and rent this house out so he can get back to school, grieve his parents and finish healing from the past."

"Or maybe he needs a new address." Tam was relentless.

"Maybe." Ali had to admit she liked the idea of having Heath as a neighbor for the long haul. In just a matter of a couple months, he'd gained a footing in Charlie's life that obviously needed to continue after he went back to school. She sighed. "Charlie will miss him in the fall."

"Maybe he can take a math class." Tam looked up from her computer screen. "Maybe you need a math class."

Ali snorted. "One and nothing don't make two," she repeated.

"What do you mean?"

"It's something Heath said to me," she explained.

"Hmm." Tam gazed out the window. "I always heard that one and one make three."

"Nope. Not in my case, anyway."

"Have it your way, but I hope you don't regret it," Tam warned. "Sometimes God has something else in mind for you. He knows your true needs."

Ali waved her off, although a nugget of concern settled in the bottom of her stomach. Did she really know what was best for herself, or did she need to take a step back and ask God? The Scripture she'd read that morning stepped to the forefront of her mind. "I know I was supposed to come to Lagrasse. I believe with a little more work and blessings, the business will take off. The Lord knows I need it, so that's my faith, and I have to trust in it."

"Like I always say, I'm proud of you," said Tam. She motioned toward the window. "Would you have a doughnut and some milk with me across the street? Mornings are always slow." Ali's stomach pitched with enthusiasm despite the fact that she couldn't spare a nickel. "My treat this time," Tam insisted before she could decline.

"Now I remember why you're my favorite cousin," Ali admitted. They laughed together as they let themselves out the door. Morning sunshine welcomed them with an alluring cloud of pastry-saturated air.

Chapter Eleven

Heath put a second coat of paint on the carport after classes on Wednesday. Trooper stayed nearby, but even with his companionship, Heath found the day a little too lonely. After checking his work, he headed for the storage room to wash off the brush, relieved to go back into the house. It was a warm day, and he was beginning to feel like a turkey slowly roasting in the oven. After calling Trooper, he went inside for something to drink and to change out of his grubby clothes. His phone buzzed as soon as he dropped it on the counter, but he ignored it, assuming it was work. Fishing for a sports drink from the fridge, he downed it and tossed the bottle into the trash just as the phone rang again. He grumbled and put off riffling through the cabinets to pick the cell phone back up. Ali's name and number scrolled across the screen. Hoping things had been resolved with Charlie, he answered, trying not to sound too eager to talk to her again. "Hi, Ali. What's up?"

On the other side of the line, he heard a small intake of air. "It's me. Yeah. Ali." She exhaled along with her name. "I'm sorry to bother you. Is Charlie there?" She waited, and concern shot through Heath at the sound of expectation in her voice.

"No, he's not. Did he say he would be?"

After a startled pause, Ali said, "I just assumed. He wasn't riding his bike in front of the house, and I walked to the edge of the woods and called, but he never came."

"Let me check," Heath offered. He hurried to the sliding glass door and peered out. There was nothing but brush piles and overgrown bushes waiting to be cut down. He scanned the pasture behind the house. It was empty. His old tire swing was still. "He's not here, and I haven't heard from him. Do you want me to come over and help you look?"

"No, that's okay," she said in a sunny voice he knew better than to believe. "I'll just check around the house one more time."

Heath didn't have kids, but he knew when something was off. "Ali, I don't mind," he insisted. "Is he still upset about me not going on the fishing trip?"

"He's over it," she said quickly. "I told him we'd bring you a souvenir."

"That's good, then," Heath replied, although it bruised his feelings that he was so easily forgotten. "Keep me posted."

"I'm sure he's around here somewhere." Ali hesitated, then said, "We did have another quarrel this afternoon when I picked him up from school. He wanted to come over and tell you he was bringing you back a souvenir, but I told him not to bother you."

"I see." Heath searched the pasture again. "Look, don't be upset with him when you find him. He didn't come over here."

"Okay. Thanks."

They disconnected, and Heath returned to the patio. The backyard was silent, the overgrown garden wilder without its chicken wire. It needed to be bushhogged. Heath wondered if he'd ever get the house up to par. Perhaps he shouldn't have been so bent on doing everything himself, but he hadn't wanted to be any trouble. At least that's what he'd said. It was really the thought of people watching him grieve. Besides, the congregation had already done so much for his mother while she was sick. This was on him. He should have been here more, he thought sadly, not just near the end. She could have told him sooner, but not wanting her boys to fuss over her, she'd kept the terminal news to herself as long as possible. Would he have come back if she'd asked? He gave a nod as he stared out across his land. Of course he would have. This was home. And for the first time in a long time, it was where he felt like he belonged, even though there wasn't a large university here. It was another equation that made no sense.

Heath regarded the lush trees in the distance, then remembered his promise to fix up the tree house before the fall semester. But there were the wasps to deal with. Perhaps that was something he should force himself to get started on, although he still had plenty to do. Was he making excuses?

Suddenly, he suspected he knew where Charlie might be and gave Trooper a whistle. The dog bounded outside to join him, and Heath slid the glass door shut. Together, they strolled through the pasture dodging fire ant hills and burrows, the dog only mildly distracted until they reached the woods. The fanning tree branches seemed to cool the air, and Trooper became more excited the farther they walked into the canopy. He dashed off for the tree house with an excited bark before Heath could stop him. When he reached the beech tree, the dog was making circles around it and whining. Heath put his hands on his hips and looked around. His gaze immediately went to the wasps' nest in the distance. It was doubled in size, and he could hear them. Dread sucked the air from his chest like a vacuum. He involuntarily took a step back and snapped his fingers. Trooper sat. A small, rosy face peered over the edge of the tree house. "Hi, Mr. Heath."

"What are you doing up there?" Heath called in a soft whisper.

"I'm hiding," came Charlie's reply. Heath could make out a bright yellow shirt lying prostrate between the rotting boards. Yellow. Bright colors attracted wasps. Fear began building in his chest no matter how much he tried to hold it at bay.

"Charlie, you need to come down from there. It's not as sturdy as it needs to be," he gulped.

"It is, too," the boy said in a muffled voice.

Heath eyed the wasps again. "We're too close to that nest. Come down right now. Your mother is looking for you."

"She's mean."

"She's not mean," Heath replied in a whisper. "She's your mother, and it's her job to tell you things you don't want to hear."

"I wanted to come to your house and see Trooper."

"You can see Trooper now," said Heath. "Come on down." He looked around and saw the dog had wandered away, not in the least bit concerned about the wasps.

Charlie tried to change the subject. "When are you going to fix the tree house?"

"There's a wasp nest," Heath began.

"We can smoke them out," Charlie finished.

Heath paused and tried to think clearly. "If you come down, I'll take care of them so we can fix the tree house."

Charlie scrunched his lips and stared back. "I promise," Heath reiterated. The thought filled him with dismay.

"You can't poison them," the boy insisted.

"We'll try the smoke," Heath said, realizing Ali would know what to do. He mentally stewed. She had enough going on, and this was his property. Maybe Monk could help.

"Do you promise?"

"Yes, I promise." Heath's neck was beginning to hurt from looking up. "Now come down. Let's go to the tire swing and talk." Trooper barked from the underbrush, and Heath flinched at the noise.

"Okay."

The swing had been the perfect temptation to lure the boy to the ground. Or maybe it was Trooper. Regardless, Heath didn't care. All he wanted was to get away from the wasps and keep Charlie safe. The boy clambered down, and Trooper returned with a chewed Frisbee in his mouth. Taking his dog by the collar, Heath gave a firm tug, and they started back through the woods, leaving the rustling trees and whining wasps behind. Charlie threw the Frisbee and laughed with delight when Trooper made a catch, then the boy made a mad dash for the tire swing as soon as they reached the pasture. Heath found himself relaxing, pulse contained. He realized he'd come within speaking distance of a wasps' nest without losing his nerve. Of course, his concern for Charlie had helped him to stay calm, but rubbing shoulders with a beekeeper who seemed to know everything about insects had taught him to be reasonable. What'd happened to him so many years ago had been terrible, but like losing someone in an accident, it was rare. He'd just been in the wrong place at the wrong time.

Trooper darted through Charlie's legs as he swung to and fro. The silly dog's antics made the boy throw his head back and chortle with glee. Heath pushed Charlie and watched the tire carry him higher and higher into the late-afternoon sunshine. When they were tired of that game, Charlie asked him to spin him in circles, and Heath obeyed. A yellow butterfly fluttered past them, and Charlie pointed at it. "That's a tiger swallowtail."

"It's beautiful."

"Do you know if you touch a butterfly, it can't fly anymore?" Charlie ducked his head to watch the ground spin under his feet.

"I do," said Heath. "It removes powder from their wings that they need to fly."

"Yes, it's like pollen, but it's not. It's tiny scales. They suck nectar out of flowers with really long tongues like this." Charlie stuck his tongue out as far as he could, and Heath laughed.

"That's a good impression. Maybe you're part butterfly."

"I wish I could fly," said the boy.

"Maybe you can take a plane ride someday."

"Yes, but I'd rather swim. Like a fish. Minnows are fast. Jellyfish eat them, though."

"That's too bad."

"It's the web of life. They sting like bees." Charlie looked up at Heath. "Are you afraid of jellyfish?"

"Not really."

"Why not? I've been stung by one."

"Did it hurt?"

"Yes, but I handled it."

Heath chuckled. "I bet you're more careful now."

"I always check the surf flag. If it's purple for wildlife, that means jellyfish most of the time."

"Do you get in the water then?"

"Nope. Even when there's not a purple flag, I check just to be safe." The boy leaned back and stared at the sky. "I told you, Mr. Heath. I'm safe. If I ever ride a motorcycle, I'll wear a helmet."

"So jellyfish don't keep you out of the ocean." Heath was impressed.

"I'll probably never get stung again unless I'm not paying attention," said Charlie.

"You're very brave."

"I'm just growing up."

"Charlie, just because we grow up doesn't mean we don't get hurt." Heath began to wind the tire swing up again because it'd wallowed to a stop.

"I know." Charlie lapped the air with his tongue again as if tasting the honeysuckle on the breeze. "But I'd rather get hurt a few times than not grow up at all. Wouldn't you?"

The innocent words penetrated Heath's heart with their truth. Getting hurt was a part of life, whether it was bee stings or a broken heart. He was suddenly grateful Charlie and Ali had moved into the old farmhouse behind his fence, although the apiary would continue to expand as Ali grew her business. It was fine, he decided. God forbid a swarm ever happened, but at least he knew not to swat or scream or run. He'd been hurt. He'd healed. He'd educated himself. He needed to be brave so he could keep growing, too. And not just when it came to bees.

"Charlie?"

"Yeah?"

"When you get back from your birthday trip, I'll be finished teaching my classes. We can start rebuilding the tree house then, okay?"

Charlie tilted his head back and found Heath's eyes with his chocolate-brown ones. He gave him an upside-down smile. "Sweet, Mr. Heath." The boy giggled as Heath let go and the tire began to twirl. Charlie shouted with delight, clutching the tire for dear life. Heath watched him spin like the years, imagining him as a teenager and then a young man. How wonderful it would be to watch Charlie grow up here in Lagrasse. It was a shame Heath would only come back and forth when he needed to deal with something as a landlord.

"Heath?" The familiar sound of Ali's voice turned his head. She emerged from the trees, and he could tell by the look on her face she was relieved to see her son. "Where have you been, Charlie? I told you that you aren't allowed on Mr. Heath's property anymore." Her voice elevated with tension. "I was really worried about you. I almost called the sheriff."

Heath interrupted her. "I'm sorry. It's my fault. I should have called and told you I found him."

She raised a brow. "I completely forgot," he admitted.

"I'm sorry he's bothering you again," she said stiffly.

"Don't be." Heath smiled, but she looked frosty.

"But you said—"

He waved her off. "I took down your fence. What did I expect?"

"Hi, Mom," Charlie said as the swing stopped again. He struggled to climb out of the tire, then gave up and flopped onto the ground like a worm.

"I told you not to leave the backyard," she repeated in a stern tone.

Charlie shot Heath a look of desperation, but Heath bit the inside of his lip to keep silent. "I'm sorry." Charlie hung his head.

She pointed. "Head straight back to the house. Now." Trooper came up and licked her hand, but she maintained her serious composure. "Homework. Now. And this was your last chance. If you disobey me one more time, there will not be a birthday trip. You scared me to death."

Charlie groaned. "Yes, ma'am."

"Trooper, stay," Heath ordered. "Bye, Charlie."

"Bye, Mr. Heath. Thanks for pushing me on the swing."

"You're welcome. Get your homework done, now. School's almost over."

Charlie gave him a parting grin that melted away under the disapproving eye of his mother. He stood up and slunk away, and Ali dropped her arms, her lips a grim line of frustration. "Once again, I am really sorry he snuck over," she said to Heath. "I don't know what to do with him."

Heath held up his hands to stop her. "Please, don't. It's no use. Trooper thinks he belongs to us." Trooper decided at that moment to jump up and rest his paws on Ali's shoulder, and Heath hurried over to pull him down. "No," he said sternly, then sighed. "I'm sorry. This dog."

She chuckled. "My boy. Same."

Heath joined her, but his amusement faded when he realized they'd both grabbed Trooper by the collar at the same time. The dog yanked away, and Heath was left holding Ali's hand. Instead of letting go, he found himself clutching it, then eyeing the soft, freckled skin on her arm that reminded him of white daylilies. He looked up and found her as still as a deer in a meadow, doe eyes guarded. But she didn't pull away. Her fingers curled around his, and they stood together in dappled sunlight studying each other as if they were two sides of the same coin, but solvable, equal, one. Heath could see them as one, he realized.

Ali looked into him with her mysterious eyes, and his heart spun so hard it sent pulses of energy to the ends of his fingertips. He hadn't felt electricity like this since…since the last time he'd fallen in love. The thought was a shot of adrenaline to his already-racing heart, but this time, Heath didn't feel the need to run or fight. He was as helpless as a bee in a garden, drawn to her sweetness that took his breath away.

He found himself swallowing for air as she eased her fingers from his hand. "Trooper," he stammered. "I should go get my dog. I think he's followed him home. Charlie, I mean."

Ali gave a quick nod. "I know. I know who you meant." She had the grace to flush, and it made her look even prettier. Heath cleared his throat and reminded himself she was Charlie's mom. And she'd been someone else's wife, who'd taken her heart with him when he passed. She had already drawn a line between them. He couldn't cross it again.

Ali was too distracted by what had transpired in the middle of the pasture to be any more irritated with Charlie. She kept her thoughts to herself while she made dinner and he did his homework at the table. Afterward, she tucked him into bed and listened while he told her about Heath's promise to rebuild the tree house after the fishing trip. With a sigh, she sat down on the edge of the bed. "There's something I have to tell you, Charlie. Okay?" The boy became solemn, and she took a deep breath. "We won't be able to stay a whole week in Florida. Maybe another time. We're only going to fish for one day, maybe two. We just didn't make enough money this spring."

"That's okay, Mom."

Ali almost teared up with gratitude. She couldn't explain the danger of maxing out a credit card and not being able to pay it off quickly to a child. Just three days in Florida would cost a small fortune. "We'll have more hives in the future," she said, "and hopefully a better vegetable garden."

"Because of Trooper?"

"Right." She sighed. "It'll be some time before I can put a fence back up, so we need to keep an eye out for him."

"I won't be able to go to the tree house if there's a new fence," said Charlie sadly.

Ali patted the blanket over his legs. "Mr. Heath won't be there anyway. Someone else will." Her son frowned. "Don't worry about it right now."

"I don't want him to leave," the boy said stubbornly.

"I don't, either, honeybee." Ali bit her tongue. She shouldn't encourage Charlie, especially when her skin burned from the lingering touch of Heath's hand and the look in his eyes—a look she knew that she'd returned even if it made no sense at all. He was a good guy. A great guy. But... "Well, good night, Charlie," she whispered, mind swimming.

"Good night, Mom." Her son turned over to his side. If only his father was here to see him grow, she thought sadly, to see him reading, writing and learning his multiplication tables. Ali thought of Trooper and the unbridled joy that shined in Charlie's eyes every time he saw the dog—and his owner. With a tumbling stomach, she turned off the light and went straight to bed to stop herself from calling Tam. She needed to talk to someone, but not her son. And not Heath, either. That wouldn't do. There was no reason for him to know the healed corners of her heart were now fertile, eager to take seed again and allow love to grow. Maybe it already had.

She shivered at the thought. Perhaps she should pray about it. Heath had sown something in her soul she thought had long grown over. He'd nourished poor and stony ground she'd believed would never produce anything again. And yet, something had bloomed inside her since he'd come to Lagrasse. She smiled more, laughed harder and, to be honest, she'd begun to dream again.

Tam was right. Ali needed more than her

honey and her child. She needed to be loved. Maybe this was the lesson God was trying to teach her. He did know what was best. But falling for a neighbor who'd been stung one too many times himself would be fruitless in the end. She'd get hurt, and this time it'd be her own fault. She prayed the good Lord knew what He was doing. She hoped the fall semester would hurry and come soon.

Chapter Twelve

Ali made a rebellious beeline for the Last Re-Torte after dropping Charlie off at school on Friday morning. The trip to Florida couldn't come fast enough, because she needed miles between Heath and her rambling thoughts. She chose two blueberry muffins, skipped the beverages to save a few dimes, then hurried across the street to the Gracious Earth. She found Tam teetering on a step stool. Tam looked over her shoulder as the bells jangled. "What do you have for me, and why aren't you saving money?"

Ali held up the bag. "I'll swap you a muffin for a cold juice," she bargained.

Tam jumped down, her shelves properly rearranged. "I'll take it. Any more honey?"

"Just the new lip balm."

Tam rushed over with her hand out. "Let me try some. I'll be your first reviewer."

Ali chuckled. "Charlie and I have been using it, and it's great. I don't have to use any other moisturizer, and his lips don't dry out."

"That's perfect. How's it taste?"

Ali held up three selections. "I went with natural flavoring drops from popular desserts—peach, key lime and strawberry."

"Mmm, that sounds delicious."

Ali handed Tam a peach sample. She pulled the lid off and rubbed it over her lips, then licked them. "This tastes great, and it's really soothing. Do you mind if I use it for a few days before I put them out?"

"No, I don't mind at all," Ali agreed.

"I'll pay you in advance," Tam insisted. "I know they'll sell."

Ali lightened. The extra money now would help. "I hope they do go fast, because I have plenty."

They discussed pricing while munching the muffins. "How about Heath?" Tam asked as if she could see him hanging around in the back of Ali's mind. "Did you have him try some?"

"No," admitted Ali. "He did like the salve, though."

"I know. He came in yesterday and picked up another tin. Did he tell you?"

Ali shook her head and pretended to study the essential oils on the shelf behind her cousin. "What?" Tam leaned closer to study her as if she had an eyelash in her eye. "Did something happen again?" Heat rushed to Ali's face, and she put a hand to her neck as if she could stop it. "Oh my goodness. What'd he say this time?"

"Nothing," croaked Ali. "He didn't do a thing."

"That's a change."

Ali forced a smile. "Charlie snuck over there again. He was mad at me, and he's obsessed with that tree house. Heath talked him down and took him to play on an old tire swing for a little while."

"Did that help?"

No, it complicated things, thought Ali. At least the feelings she'd been trying to ignore. They'd gone from persistent to undeniable. "It calmed Charlie down."

"And your face is red because...?" Tam stared, and Ali regretted that her cousin knew her so well. She felt the flush deepen and forced a nonchalant laugh.

"I don't know." She put an elbow on the counter and planted her chin in the palm of her hand. "He just..." Ali cleared her throat. "After I sent Charlie home, I stayed behind, and we talked for a few minutes, and I guess...something..."

Ali suddenly felt feverish. She was rambling. "I realized how much we really get along and like each other."

"You care about him."

Ali fanned her cheeks. "It's hard not to. The

guy works with young people, is a fierce dog lover and treats Charlie like—"

"His son?"

"Yeah." Ali wrenched her lips. "What happens when he leaves? Or if…"

"You're falling for the guy." Tam smiled.

Ali felt her shoulder blades tighten. "No," she said stubbornly. "It's only been four years. Besides, Heath's been married before, too, and he's gun-shy. Not to mention, we could never make it work between my bees and his job at the university."

Tam raised a brow. "You wouldn't move?"

Ali shook her head. "We've just rooted our feet. Charlie's happy here. I'm happy. You're here." She looked at Tam with determination. "I've just started the next chapter of my life and gotten used to the idea of raising my son on my own."

Tam frowned. "No amount of love and loyalty means not moving on with your life. You could have someone again if you took a risk, and you know Keith would understand."

"Starting a honey business was risky enough, and you know how that's going," argued Ali. She exhaled with frustration. "Not that you weren't right. Things somehow worked out for an edited version of Charlie's birthday trip."

"I told you so."

"Yes, and the summer looks promising. The salsa garden is coming along, the melon seedlings are gorgeous and the new hives look good."

"How much do you think you'll get this year?" asked Tam.

"I'm hoping for a hundred pounds per hive. The new ones are really important since I lost two to mites this spring."

"I hope it works out."

"Me, too," said Ali. "I'll need to pay off Charlie's birthday trip as soon as possible to avoid the credit card interest, though." She looked down at the stacks of lip balm on the counter. "Sometimes I feel like I'm robbing Peter to pay Paul."

Tam smiled. "It's like that for some years with a small business, but hang in there."

"I made a big mistake using the house as collateral," admitted Ali. "I need to get out from under this debt."

"All in good time. Look how far you've come."

Tam was right. Charlie was doing well, the apiary was thriving and the bank had reluctantly agreed to an extension when she'd gathered the courage to ask. She had a great community, a best friend and a wonderful neighbor in Heath. Her heart took a step back. A neighbor she could not fall for. "All I want right now is for Charlie to have a wonderful birthday and for us to be able to feed ourselves."

Tam held up a tube of lip balm. "These will sell fast. You keep at it, and you'll be able to go commercial in no time. Maybe even hire help."

"I can hardly imagine that," gushed Ali. "I never thought I could make my dreams come true all by myself."

Tam patted her hand. "Even when you feel alone, someone is always watching out for you. I told you moving to Lagrasse could change your life."

"You were right." Ali sighed with contentment. She thought of Charlie aching for his dad and his fixation on Heath. "Mostly," she amended. Father or not, Heath had been a blessing for Charlie, and she needed to let him be a part of their lives as long as he was good to her son. She'd just have to keep her wavering emotions at bay.

Ali gave Tam a hug goodbye and drove home in high spirits. Being a widow didn't mean having to struggle or be on her own; windows had opened after the most important door in her life had slammed shut. She smiled to herself as she cruised along the highway, now bordered with sparkling daisies and vibrant yellow wingstem. Life was good. Feeling renewed, she thanked God for family and friends as pulled into the drive of the farmhouse. Once out of the car, she stopped to appreciate the view of the late-morning sun spotlighting her sprawling acreage then she let herself into the backyard to check on the bees. She took two steps before she saw a frantic cloud of swarming insects in the apiary. Frowning, Ali scanned the yard for Trooper. One of the new hives was wild with activity. She hurried closer but stopped in horror when she saw wax speckled around its entrance, which meant there were raiders. Panic seized her. She spun about to check the rest of the apiary and saw another one under attack. An enormous insect buzzed by, and she jumped back. Wasps!

Ali ran to the back door for her bee suit. She managed to climb into it while tripping over her own feet, grabbed her hat and veil, and dashed back outside to the distressed hive. It was engulfed by enemies. Pulse flying, Ali searched for any guard bees. Her new hives weren't as strong as the older ones, and losing them would be a disaster. She cringed over putting off extra precautions until her income became more stable. Robbing screens could have prevented this.

Ali saw dollar signs. The fishing trip. She couldn't go through with it. Heart sinking, she stumbled away to watch in despair as the wasps ravaged her new bees and plundered her sweet gold. The entrances were too big. She ran for the hose, accepting she'd have to replace the colonies, but it was urgent to stop the thieving wasps before they moved on to another hive. Tears filled her eyes as she watched the honeybees fight for survival. With a rock in her chest, Ali knew even if she found more credit, she couldn't take a trip right now. It was too risky. The invaders would come back and test another hive. She needed to police the apiary, to reinforce the entrances. Yes, they had queens, but she was their custodian after Mother Nature.

With a knot in her throat, Ali realized she could not keep her promise to her son. Then there was the loss of product she'd counted on for the summer. Losing one hive after another would make it impossible to make any payments. She would lose the business. Her home. Everything.

Tears began to stream as she choked back the bitterness of failure. Why had she let herself believe God was on her side, she wondered in despair. Was it blind faith? She'd been a fool. Now she'd have to start over. Again. That meant going back to work somewhere else, which would separate her from her already-fatherless son.

And God had said He knew what she needed.

A knock at his door startled Heath, but he jumped up from his desk, thankful for a break from grading assignments. His heart thumped with hope that it was Ali, but he didn't hope Charlie had broken his promise again. Feeling his brow furrow, Heath pulled open the door, and to his surprise, he found Charlie standing beside Tam with his eyes the size of quarters. Tam was not her usual smiling or teasing self, either. She ran her hand over her hair to smooth it down, but it looked more like a gesture of distress.

"Is everything okay?" Heath reached for Charlie on instinct, and the boy wrapped his small arms around Heath's waist. "What's wrong?" On cue, Trooper appeared, snuffling tenderly as if feeling the tension.

Tam's lips were set in a grim line. "Ali asked me to pick up Charlie. A swarm of wasps attacked one of the new hives and has started on a second one."

Heath felt the blood drain from his head. The world began to shift in and out of focus. "Wasps?" he repeated as if he'd heard her wrong. Charlie let out a muffled whimper.

"Yes." Tam groaned. "She didn't check them closely yesterday, and it looks like they've been going at it for a while."

"That's terrible." Heath tried not to picture thousands of bees and wasps in battle. Perspiration broke out across his shoulder blades. "Is she okay? Is she safe?"

"Yes, she's okay. Physically." Tam nodded toward Charlie. "Can you keep him? I'm going to help."

"I—of course." Heath felt guilty at the relief that rushed over him. He could watch Charlie and keep him safe, but Ali… Losing the new hives meant less honey for her in the long run. Suddenly, Heath felt a surge of protectiveness and an urgency to fight. She couldn't lose her bees. She'd lose her home. "Maybe Charlie can stay with Trooper."

"No," Charlie cried. "I want to help, too!"

"I'm not sure there's much we can do," said Tam. "She's running sprinklers, but she said it's a sizable swarm."

Wasps. Swarming. Heath thought he was going to faint.

"It's probably the tree house wasps," Charlie growled.

Tam looked at Heath curiously. "Tree house wasps?"

"There's a pretty big nest on my property. I meant to…" Heath faltered. "I was going to take care of it while they were in Florida." *Somehow.* He felt sick. He should have faced his fears. Now they were someone else's problem. "Come on," he said, stepping out and nudging Trooper back. "Charlie, you have to promise to stay in the car or go into your house."

"Okay," Charlie agreed as Heath guided him toward the carport with Tam following from behind.

"Are you sure about this?" she asked in a wary tone.

"I am." Heath took a deep breath. He gave Charlie a weak smile. "Charlie's science fair project helped me a lot. I've learned so much about bees lately, I'm not afraid." It was a small fib, he knew, but there was some truth to it. Some faith. He gave Charlie a confident nod. "I'm not scared."

"Me, neither," said Charlie. "I'm not afraid because Mom said we have to take good care of them for our family."

"Don't worry," Heath assured him. He helped Charlie into the back of his car and buckled him in with trembling hands while Tam hurried to her small van. Heath took Charlie by the chin and looked him in the eyes. "Everything's going to be okay. We're going to fix this, and we're going to do it safely." The boy gave him a courageous nod, and Heath's heart filled with boundless love for the little boy he knew he would never let down again.

Ali sat on the back porch, swallowed up in the extra-large bee suit, feeling hot and defeated. It was an awful combination. Her throat hurt from trying to control the grief that wanted to rip her in half. She knew she'd matured since enduring the loss of a man who was everything to her and her child, but at the moment, she was barely holding it together. She was supposed to be the optimist in the crowd, a champion of the weak and a cheerleader of the downtrodden, but another insurmountable mountain had risen before her, and she was blindsided, disappointed and exhausted. How could God let life dig another pit when she'd just crawled her way out of the last one? She'd never felt as at home as she did in Lagrasse. This was supposed to be it. She exhaled and stared at the land that belonged to her—at least until she couldn't pay off the loan and credit card. Here she'd been worrying about missing a month, but her entire honey crop was in danger. What had she been thinking, taking such a risk? It had been as foolish as hopping onto a motorcycle without a helmet, as reckless as speeding down a one-lane country road. She put her head in her hands and whimpered.

"Mom!" The sound of Charlie's voice should have been comforting, but Ali's stomach flopped over with dread. She'd already asked for an extension, and she couldn't fit anymore of the vacation to Florida on the credit card than she already had. She tried to rearrange the defeat on her face.

"Hey, honeybee," she said in a quiet voice. She held out her arms, and he ran to her, nearly toppling her over. When she settled him onto her lap, she realized he was not alone. Tam and Heath had come around the corner. Tam's eyes were round with concern, Heath's with discomfort. Ali slid Charlie to the step beside her and climbed to her feet. "You guys didn't have to come."

Tam wrapped her in a hug, and to her surprise, Heath stepped forward, too. Ali gave him a hesitant embrace, then backed away, knowing she must smell dirty and sour.

"Are you okay?" Heath searched her face.

She gave him a slight nod, gritting her teeth so she didn't break down. "I'll figure it out," she said bravely.

"How bad is it, really?" Tam demanded.

"Wow!" Charlie's exclamation said it all.

Ali watched Heath's pupils swell and followed his gaze to the wild swarm in the southwest corner of the backyard. "Don't worry," she said, touching his arm. "They won't come over here. We don't have any honey." She sank back onto the back porch stairs glumly. Charlie hopped down to the grass. "Stay here, bee."

He grabbed a porch post and hung there, swinging back and forth. "Are they killing them?"

"I suppose," Ali sighed. "But they're really after the honey and larvae."

"Can't be much in those with the hives being

new," said Tam. She dropped onto the stairs beside her. Heath walked off the porch and went over to stand by Charlie.

"What about the other ones?" asked Heath, looking over his shoulder.

"That's what I'm worried about. They go for the weakest first. The most vulnerable," explained Ali. Her voice crackled, and Heath crossed the distance between them in three strides. He sat down on the other side of her, sandwiching her between Tam and himself, and though her entire life was falling apart, Ali felt a smidge better. She gave him a weak smile, and something that looked like regard in his eyes made her think he might kiss her. It made her forget everything going wrong for a split second, but there were more important problems.

He took her hand. "I'm really sorry, Ali. This is my fault."

"Now, Heath, don't say that." Tam shooed his words away.

"What do you mean?"

"The wasps." Heath's voice was low, sorrowful. Ali squinted in confusion. "There's a giant wasp nest on my property by the tree house," said Heath. "That's why I didn't want Charlie running back and forth."

Ali stiffened. "A wasp nest? Why didn't you say so?"

"Didn't I? I thought Charlie would have mentioned it."

"He wouldn't have thought anything about it. I wish…" She faltered. It wasn't like she could have done anything. It wasn't on her land.

Heath huffed in frustration. "I meant to ask around about any professionals. I mean, that was the plan while you and Charlie went to Florida, because I promised him we'd fix the tree house."

"It's too late now," Ali choked. "I'm not sure what the damage will be once I get in there, but I'm going to have to start all over and hope they don't bother any of the healthy colonies."

"I'm so sorry," Heath repeated.

"There's no way I can take Charlie on this fishing trip now," Ali said in a quiet voice so her son didn't hear. "I've got to see to this, and I can't risk putting anything else on credit that I may not be able to pay off." She knew she was unloading on him, but she couldn't stop herself. "Why didn't you just ask me about it?"

Heath bowed his head. "I should have. I didn't want it to be your problem."

"I would have taken more precautions," Ali said with bitterness. He looked away, and it jabbed her with guilt, but her home—her life— was on the line. And that mattered more than her heart.

"I'm sure you'll come up with something," Tam encouraged her.

"We'll help," promised Heath.

"You've done enough," Ali replied, wishing it didn't sound like an indictment.

"What do you mean?"

They stared at one other, and Ali's frustration spun out of control. "If you would have told me about them, I could have dealt with it," she said in exasperation.

Heath's face paled. "I was getting the nerve up to deal with it, but I was going to get it done."

"Well, your nerves destroyed my crop for the year," Ali muttered.

"If you'd let me look over your accounts, I could have helped."

"I told you I don't need a bookkeeper," she shot back. "I'm as good at math as anybody else. Besides, you're going back to school after the summer. You're not a local accountant." She saw him flinch but didn't stop to ask herself why. "If the fence was…" Ali stopped, realizing what she was saying was ridiculous. The fence would not have prevented the wasps from attacking her hives. It would have only prevented Charlie from traipsing over to Heath's whenever he felt like it—and kept her from caring for someone. But she couldn't care for Heath. This proved it.

"Charlie!" Tam called suddenly. She got up

to her feet. "Come on, let's get you started on homework before I have to pick up Piper from soccer."

Charlie looked back with reluctance and darted his attention to Ali. He seemed more entertained than upset, clueless as to what this all really meant. "I want to watch the swarm."

Ali gave her head a small shake. "Go on in with Tam," Heath said sternly. "Your mom's upset and needs a minute."

Charlie gave all three adults a scowl and sauntered over, patting Ali on the shoulder in a very adult gesture as he trudged up the stairs to the back door. Her eyes teared, and she swiped at them. To see Charlie do as Heath requested because he respected and adored him tore at her heart.

"Are you okay? Really okay?" Heath murmured, once Tam's and Charlie's footsteps faded away. "Please forgive me for not thinking to mention the wasps to you. I didn't realize this kind of thing could happen. Maybe I can help with Charlie's birthday trip."

He reached for her hand, but Ali eased it out of reach. She and the accounting professor needed a new line of demarcation. "No," she said firmly. "I think we've paid each other back enough. He's just going to have to deal with the heartache like he had to when his father passed away." She pulled up her hair to wipe off her damp neck and keep her hands busy. "We can't afford a big trip right now."

"Maybe you can get another extension."

"I don't dare risk it. I'm already worried about asking this month."

"I'm really sorry about the wasps."

"So am I." Ali steadied her trembling self. "You should get back on home, Heath. I know you have a lot to do with finals and all. You didn't have to come." She took a deep breath and hardened her heart. It was time to be crystal clear. "Really, you didn't. I will lock Charlie in the house if that's what I have to do to keep him from coming over anymore."

"You don't have to do that." Heath frowned.

"I think it's best," she said, unable to meet his eyes. "I think it's best if…" Her cheeks flamed with remorse, and she hoped he'd think it was just from the stuffiness of her bee suit. "I think it's best if you keep your distance. From Charlie, I mean…and me."

Heath looked surprised. His gaze traveled from her eyes to her mouth, and the bubbly twinge she'd felt when she'd wondered if he'd kiss her came back. She gave him a tight smile. "I know you've been stung before and you certainly don't want to go through something like that again." She waved toward the hives. "I have a business to tend to and my son to raise. You've done enough, and I'm grateful for it, but I don't want Charlie to get the wrong idea."

Heath sat motionless, as if stunned for a few seconds, then shot to his feet like he'd been pinched. "You're right," he agreed. His voice sounded cold, emotionless. "I better get back home and finish up my classes." His receding footfalls echoed on the floorboards behind her, hurting Ali's heart. Then they stopped. "Don't worry about the wasps after today," said Heath. "Once they get back to the nest, I'll find someone to come out tomorrow, even if I have to hire out of state. Then I'll start on a fence." Ali looked over her shoulder. Heath was staring at her with a blank face. "You won't have to worry about any intruders in your apiary anymore," he promised. "Goodbye, Ali."

She tried to nod her thanks, but his words were scalding. She knew there was more behind them than neighborly concern. He left abruptly, and she felt tears wet her eyes as she dropped her head into her hands to suppress a piercing headache. A fence? Her and her boundaries. Heath and his. He was a well-respected professor doing what he loved but couldn't find the recognition he craved in a small town. The messy property was just an excuse. He'd set up a wall between them the first time they'd met, and she'd matched it. But the wall had come down. Why had she thrown it back up? And why had he agreed it needed to be there?

Bees buzzed frantically in the distance, and Ali tried not to picture the loss of her drones and the workers who'd tried to establish themselves. Then there was the poor queen, trying to do it all, to control everything around her when she really had no control. And she was all alone. Ali's eyes pooled over, and she didn't fight the tears this time. A sob erupted, and she put the back of her hand over her mouth.

Tam appeared from out of nowhere and dropped down beside her. She threw an arm around her shoulder. "Don't cry, Ali. You always manage anything life throws at you."

Ali nodded miserably. "At me, yes," she said in a strangled voice. "But at my heart? I don't know."

Tam looked toward the corner of the house. "Where's Heath?" Ali forced back another sob, almost choking on it. She gave her head a small shake. "Oh, honey," whispered Tam, guessing exactly what had transpired. "What did you do?"

Chapter Thirteen

Heath tossed and turned all night, his mind trying to work out equations that had no answers. He woke up exhausted on Saturday morning but dressed and sent out the final grades for the semester before perusing his emails. A message from the head of the department stopped him in his tracks. A professor had a family emergency, and an instructor was needed on campus for a summer class. Was he interested? Heath tensed so hard it pinched his back. He left the email on the screen and pushed away from the desk. Was he?

Desperate for distraction, he marched outside to evaluate the rest of the yard work left to be done. He tried to ignore a marble boulder in his chest with Ali's face carved in it and focus on his chores. He'd accomplished a great deal, with the exception of mowing regularly and grading over the garden still trying to claw its way back from neglect. There was nothing major left except the overgrown trees and the roof repair. He looked around and strained his ears to see if he heard any humming sounds, then relaxed. All was well. At least at his house.

He ran through the remaining figures left over from his inheritance and hoped they would cover the deductible for the roof. Monk had recommended someone the last time they'd spoken. Thinking of his old friend, Heath wondered if he should make the trip to the farmers market to join him. There were still boxes of antique mixing bowls and bakeware to sell, but the thought of chatting with other people that might include Ali and Charlie made him feel miserable. Somehow in their battle over property lines, her bees and his mischievous dog, he'd bonded with Ali and her son, but like in his nightmares, the equation did not work. They both knew that it was better to put a stopper in whatever was budding between them to stave off any harm, although he knew in the deepest recess of his heart that it was too late for him. She'd been the brave one.

He studied a dusty bedroom window, startling when a buzzing sound echoed in his ear. Resisting the urge to swat at whatever it was, Heath took a step back and searched the air to find a curious honeybee giving him a serious evaluation. He moved out of reach again, but the assertive creature matched the distance and flew in circles around him, continuing its examination. Heath put his faith in Charlie and the bee project. Logic and reason said the insect was merely curious because of what he wore or what he smelled like. He regretted his choice of fragrant deodorant and cologne and decided some of Tam's unscented soaps would be a better choice if he was going to live here...

Live here? Would he ever? Perhaps. Yes. It'd always been in the back of his mind. That's why he'd agreed with his brother not to sell the place. Not just for their parents or nostalgia. It was a part of him. Some inner instinct had always whispered life would bring him full circle to Lagrasse, and he'd certainly never been against it. He'd been happy here. He could be happy again. But for now, he was committed to the fall semester, and the head of the department had contacted him about the summer class on campus. If he were to return to Auburn right now, no one in Lagrasse would miss him. Except maybe Charlie. There was no reason to stay in town and continue to fall for Charlie's mother. Heath sighed. That's what was happening. He knew it.

The curious honeybee lost interest and departed for the lilies blooming in the overgrown flower beds against the back of the house. Heath wondered which colony it belonged to, then remembered the destroyed hives. No home. No family. Perhaps the bee was lost.

He scanned the dilapidated roof. The university town was his address, but it'd never felt like a permanent haven where he had family that had his back and loved him unconditionally. He'd thought he'd have that when he got married, but things didn't come together. It'd never been in his heart to move to Nevada, and he should have been more forthcoming or just bitten the bullet and packed up his things. But what was done was done. The problem was, he'd let himself ease into a routine here in Lagrasse, when his only purpose for coming home was to fix up the house and rent it out. Not carry on like he intended to stay.

Heath choked back a snort. Only numbers ever made sense, and he should stick to them. He thought of the job offer and wondered if the roof would wait until fall. He could return at the end of the summer term for a short time and leave before he built up any of Charlie's expectations.

Charlie. The boy wouldn't be going deep-sea fishing. Heath's stomach sank. He'd also promised Charlie he'd fix the tree house, but if he left for campus now... Heath wagged his head in frustration over the decisions needing to be made while he eyed the roof. There were no new leaks, so it wasn't an immediate need. He chewed his lip. If insurance covered most of it...

With a deep breath, Heath whipped out his

phone and worked through some numbers on the calculator app. He looked up at the gutters and nodded to himself. Yes, Charlie would be disappointed if he left earlier than expected, but he could still give the boy something that would cheer him up—a memorable birthday and a nice goodbye.

Heath hurried back into the house to make a few phone calls and then, with a prayer and a plan, headed out with Trooper at his heels carrying an armful of two-by-fours and his toolbox.

Monk arrived an hour later. Heath wiped his temples and stood up, eyeing the busy wasp nest several trees over while stretching away the tension between his shoulder blades. Monk waved as he approached.

"Decided to fix this up, huh?"

"Yes." Heath motioned at what he'd accomplished so far.

"Looks like you just need some plywood, a few more beams and some shingles."

"Plywood was what I hoped you'd have. The shingles will have to wait."

"You'll probably have some left over from the roofers."

"That's the plan—eventually. I don't want to do too much or get too loud right now."

Monk eyed the wasp nest. It was the size of

a watermelon—from a horror movie. "So that's the problem over there, huh?"

"Yeah." Heath motioned toward the Harding property. "I don't know how many hives they've gotten into but at least a couple."

"That's a shame." Monk's bushy brows lowered to his eyes. "When are the pest control people going to be here?"

"This afternoon. The one you recommended from south of Atlanta is coming down. They said it'd be about dusk and to make sure most of the wasps are back in the nest."

"Are you sure you don't want to take care of it ourselves?" Monk looked ready for the challenge, but Heath whipped his head back and forth.

"Just working on the tree house with them nearby is a big step for me. I'm going to pay the professionals to handle the nest. I appreciate you letting me come over for a couple days until I'm sure the wasps are gone."

Monk shrugged his thick shoulders. "You know we don't mind. I'm glad you're taking care of it. They'd be back next year after the winter, too."

"I didn't want to deal with it because I pictured them swarming my house if someone bothered their nest. I didn't even think about Ali's hives."

"Yes. It's sad." Monk put his hands on his hips. "Well, hop down off that ladder, son, and let me give you a break. I'm ready to use my new electric drill on something." Heath winced but climbed down, hoping the man worked quietly. He held the ladder as Monk climbed it. "When did you talk to Ali last?" Monk asked.

"Yesterday. She was so upset I don't want to bother her anymore."

"I don't think you're bothering her," said Monk. He shifted his bulk onto the remnants of the tree house landing, and Heath passed up a narrow piece of plywood. Monk studied Heath when their eyes met. "I think she enjoys your company as much as Charlie does." Together, they set the board in place.

"I thought she did, too," Heath admitted.

"What happened?"

All at once, everything packaged so neatly inside Heath's heart unfurled in a wild, tangled rush. "We're good when we're together and have a lot more in common than you'd think. We also like the same music, dogs, kids—and pizza, of course."

Monk chuckled. "And the farmers market."

Heath nodded. "Yes, we both enjoy hanging out there on the weekends. I also like that where I'm a little slow to make a decision, she just gets ready and dives in. We kind of fit. Like magnets."

"Or a math problem," said Monk generously.

"I don't know." Heath shook off his sudden enthusiasm. "When you add up everything we've gone through on top of what we have going on in life right now, it doesn't seem to even out."

"Who says it has to be even?" Monk drove in the first screw with his electric drill, and Heath was grateful it wasn't a pounding hammer. He sneaked a look at the wasps, who seemed docile. They were probably stuffed with honey.

"That's how it works, right?" wondered Heath. "A good relationship has to add up, be even."

Monk snorted as he reached for another screw. "Heath, if you think a perfect marriage is equally balanced and comes out perfectly on both sides every time, you've got another thing coming."

"What do you mean?" Heath looked up in surprise.

"There's always a mistake. Something leftover, undone. Sometimes she does more. Sometimes I do more. We both fall short at different times, but we do the best we can. And when that happens, you forgive and work it out until the next problem comes along. It's a never-ending process. A constant balancing act, like spinning plates."

"Oh," said Heath, suddenly seeing something beyond the numbers.

Monk drilled in another screw, then sat up. "It makes you a better person in the long run. That's why we need partners—mates." He grinned at him. "Our queen bees."

"You're right," Heath agreed, unable to meet his friend's eye. "I do need someone. I need to start looking again and quit hiding in my classes." Sadness echoed through him.

Monk tilted his head. "Do you really need to look that far? What about what you've started over there?" He hooked his thumb over his shoulder toward the Hardings' place.

"Um…no," said Heath, trying to disguise his disappointment. If he didn't know better, he'd think his heart was broken again, or at least chipped or stung. "She's had a match—she has a family. I don't think she's interested in doing that again."

Monk made a noise of amusement. "Have you asked?"

"She's made it pretty clear." Heath tried to change the subject. "Did I tell you I've decided to put off replacing the roof? I'm going to pay for Charlie's birthday present so he can go fishing."

Monk laughed out loud. "You are? And have you told Miss Independent?"

"No," admitted Heath. "That's what I need you for. The tree house was just an excuse." He grinned and pointed at the wasp nest. "Plus, you're a bigger target, and I run faster."

Ali dropped off Charlie at school on Monday morning with the promise to return in time for the awards program. Her mind swam as she hurried back home to check the apiary. She'd taped the entrances to the hives while waiting for the traps to arrive, which would hopefully keep the wasps away from the other colonies, but they weren't foolproof. Charlie's disappointment over the canceled birthday trip was palpable. They'd both been so upset they'd skipped church, but Ali knew deep down it was because she didn't want to see Heath again.

She sat at her computer in the kitchen nook, staring at spreadsheets and trying to make the numbers work, but paying off the loan a year from now if last year's honey crop numbers repeated themselves did not look plausible even if she ate rice and beans, burned candles for electricity and rode a bicycle to town. She itched with frustration. As expected, a reply from the insurance company said the loss was not covered by her liability plan. She let out a tired breath. There was no choice but to find an outside job, perhaps at the local plant nursery, and she'd have to start right away. That meant finding childcare for Charlie. Her heart withered. It was something she'd never wanted to do, the whole reason she'd decided to pursue a small business. Charlie would be crushed to have to spend summer in day care on top of missing out on his birthday trip, but she had an extension penalty to cover on top of the loan now. Their next-door neighbor popped into her mind. She'd been so heartbroken over the bees, she'd pushed him away, and that had hurt her just as badly. But it was for the best. He didn't need a ready-made family, and she wasn't convinced she could risk any more pieces of her healing heart right now.

The doorbell rang, and she wondered why she hadn't heard a car. Hopping up, she was surprised to find Tam and Monk at her front door, each with toothy grins. They looked like cats who knew exactly what had happened to the canary. "Yes?"

"Can we come in?" asked Tam.

"Of course, but why?"

"We're on our lunch break," said Tam.

"I asked Tam to come," Monk admitted.

Curious, Ali motioned for them to follow her. She led them to the kitchen and pointed toward the barstools, then opened the fridge. "Share a seven-layer dip with me," she begged, pulling out a dish of leftover refried beans, guacamole and more, then she grabbed the bag of tortilla chips off the top of the fridge.

"That looks delicious," Tam declared. Monk rubbed his hands together.

"So what's up?" Ali demanded as her two guests dived into the appetizer. She leaned forward on her elbows.

"Word got around about the wasps and all that," Tam said after a few crunches.

"I'm really sorry you lost some hives," said Monk.

"It's not over yet," said Ali. "How'd you hear about it?"

"From Heath. We fixed up his old tree house."

"Already?"

The man nodded.

"What about the wasp nest nearby?"

"They came out and sprayed yesterday," said Monk.

"How did that go over? Is Heath okay?"

"I offered to let him stay at my house for a day, but in the end he refused. The wasps are gone."

"I'll still have to keep an eye out," sighed Ali.

"That was kind of him with all the work he has going on at his place," Tam said. "The tree house is safe now. Right?" She turned to Monk.

Monk nodded, his gaze locked on Ali. "We replaced some boards, so you won't have to worry about Charlie climbing up there and getting hurt."

She reached for a chip. "I wonder if Heath would mind."

Tam raised her brows with amusement. "Why do you think he did it?"

Ali couldn't help but smile. "You're right. I'll have to thank him. Charlie's just devastated that I canceled the fishing trip, so he'll be happy he can play over there again."

"It's understandable, the fishing trip," said Tam. She gave Monk the side-eye, and they both grinned.

"What?" Ali narrowed her eyes. "Unless one of you has a couple hundred gallons of honey in your back pocket, I'm going to have to figure this out myself."

"Haven't you figured out enough on your own?" asked Tam.

"What do you mean? I'm the mom, and Keith promised him the trip."

"We mean you've figured out how to work through your grief and to survive," said Monk. "You moved, bought a home, started a business and you're raising your son. And you're doing a wonderful job of it, by the way. But let your neighbors and friends help you."

Ali's heart tugged. "I knew moving to Lagrasse would bless my life, and this is a wonderful town, but I can't accept help with financial decisions I've made. They're my responsibility."

"The wasps were an act of nature," Tam argued. "We want to help you. Everyone does. The congregation chipped in."

"What?" Ali straightened in surprise.

Monk pulled out a cashier's check and pushed it across the table. "This is an anonymous donation for Charlie's eighth birthday."

The amount was generous. It'd easily cover the trip. "I can't take that," Ali choked.

"You'll hurt people's feelings if you don't, and deny them blessings," Monk warned. He wagged a finger at her. "It's for Charlie, too."

"But it's just a trip," Ali protested. "There're so many other people in need."

"And there always will be," Monk reminded her. "People who care about you and Charlie want to do this for you in memory of your husband and to honor you for trying to keep his promise. It doesn't have to be advertised. It's an anonymous gift from friends."

Ali's pulse echoed in her ears. God had come through. Again. She suddenly felt ashamed for doubting Him.

"I know it doesn't save the new hives, and you still have your loan to deal with, but take a break," counseled Monk. "You need it. Charlie does, too. Accept the money and go to Florida. Give your credit card a break."

Tears spilled over Ali's eyes, and she cupped

her face with her hands to wipe them away. "Y'all would do this for someone who's only lived here a few years?"

"You mean someone who gives to every cause?" said Monk. "Who donates to the food pantry, signs up for meal trains and worships at church with her community? Someone who cheers up her friends, reaches out to her neighbors and supports local businesses?"

Ali dropped her hands to her sides, cheeks blazing. "My goodness. I'm not a saint. Everyone tries their best, and I'm unable to do half that."

"You do more than you realize," Monk insisted. "Just because you aren't giving back full-time to everyone, everywhere, doesn't make you any less worthy of help than someone who can. It's okay to receive. You don't always have to be the giver."

"It's a colony," said Tam. "Welcome to Lagrasse."

Ali smiled as more tears coursed down her cheeks. She wiped them away and checked the clock over the stove. "I can't thank you enough. I thought going to Charlie's awards ceremony today was going to be depressing. School is almost out, and I'm going to have to hire a sitter and get a job."

Tam smiled. "This will make up for it."

Ali circled the bar to embrace her friends.

For the first time in a long time, she didn't feel alone. She thought of Heath and all he'd done for Charlie, too. Glancing at the check again, she wondered how much he'd donated. She instinctively knew he wouldn't have hesitated. "It takes a village," she murmured with wet eyes.

"And a hive mind," said Tam. Monk groaned as they broke into tearful giggles.

Chapter Fourteen

It was a blissful moment. The breeze swirled through the branches. Warm sunshine turned the insides of his eyelids pink. Heath listened to Charlie's laughter as he threw Trooper's ball as far as he could from their perch in the tall beech tree. Monk had helped Heath take the rest of the old tree house roof down, and he wondered if it even needed it at all. The platform was safe enough with its new sturdy railing, and there was a beautiful three-hundred-and-sixty-degree view.

"Mr. Heath. Hey, Mr. Heath?"

Heath opened his eyes to find Charlie leaning over him. The boy snickered. "Are you asleep on my jet?"

Heath laughed and scooted up. "No, sir. I was just resting my eyes."

"You're under arrest," Charlie declared, and they both laughed.

"Good thing it's not a ship, or you'd throw me in the hold," said Heath.

"Or make you walk the plank, but I think flying is best." Charlie peered over the side of the tree house. "Do you think we could hang the tire swing on here?"

Heath scanned a branch overhead. "I think that's a great idea."

"When I get back, okay?" said Charlie.

Heath gave two thumbs-up. Neither Charlie nor his mother had guessed where the majority of the money for their trip had come from. Heath knew it would have made his parents proud he'd given a little boy a special birthday wish instead of putting a new roof on the house. They would have agreed that tenants could wait. Heath smiled to himself.

Someone called Charlie's name, and it swam along the breeze. "That's my mom," Charlie sighed. "Tell her it's safe."

"I already did." Heath followed Charlie down the new ladder. Trooper came loping from the woods at Heath's whistle. He had not been at the Hardings'. As Charlie began walking toward home, Trooper followed after him, but he stopped when Heath called him back with a crooked finger. At the same moment, Ali came through the trees calling Charlie again. Heath's heart somersaulted. She was wearing blue slacks and a silk blouse the color of mint ice cream. He braced himself. He'd only had the nerve to text her about the tree house being open for business.

Ali came to a stop when Charlie raced up to her. She glanced at the tree house, then saw Heath standing below it. "Hello," she said, strangely formal.

Heath felt his resolve to be nothing but neighborly harden. "Hi, Ali," he said in a disconnected tone. "I was packing my car and came to look for Trooper."

"And he found me!" Charlie announced. He pointed at the tree house. "It's cool, right?"

Ali gave it a cryptic examination. "It's safe," Heath promised. "I mean, unless he jumps out of the tree." He looked at Charlie. "But he's smarter than that."

"I know," drawled Charlie. "I'm almost eight."

"You need to get back home and clean up, Charlie." Ali motioned toward the house.

"Okay. Bye, Mr. Heath."

"Have a great time, Charlie." Heath turned back to Ali before the boy was out of sight. "Are you leaving for Florida tonight?"

"Tomorrow. I, uh…" Ali looked down at her dressy clothes. "I had an interview today."

"A job interview?" said Heath in confusion. "For what?"

"For assistant manager at the plant nursery."

Heath faltered. "But what about…"

"It's no big deal," said Ali in a rush. "I'm just going to go back to work for a while. Charlie can come with me on short shifts and stay with Piper and her babysitter on long days."

Heath frowned. "What about your hives?"

"I'll work on them in the evenings and on my days off." She exhaled as if already exhausted. "Charlie can help."

"He didn't tell me about that."

"He doesn't know yet," Ali admitted. "I thought I'd talk to him about it after his birthday trip." She slanted her head. "What are you packing up for?"

"Um…" Heath hesitated. "I thought you'd heard by now." Wasn't Lagrasse a small town?

"I've been busy." Ali sounded concerned.

Heath took a deep breath, knowing she'd be relieved to hear the news. "I was offered a summer class to teach on campus. I'm going to head back now instead of the fall."

She stared, frozen. "Weren't you going to say goodbye?" Her voice sounded faint.

"I told Charlie," Heath explained, suddenly anxious. "I said he could call me when he got back and tell me about the trip."

"He doesn't seem upset," said Ali, looking relieved.

Heath chuckled. "I hope he's not." The real truth scraped the inside of his chest. Actually, it hurt. "I'll be back for a couple weeks in August to see the roof gets replaced and put the house up for rent."

Ali looked puzzled. "You're going to wait that long?"

Heath hesitated. He didn't want her to feel like she owed him anything. Ever. Not after she'd helped him so much by welcoming him back to his own hometown—and his life. She'd even inspired him to return to church. "The leak inside is fixed for now. Monk will check on the house once a week, and I hired a lawn service to keep the grass cut."

"It sounds like you have it worked out." Ali pressed her lips together. He wondered if she'd miss him, but she was the one who'd suggested he keep his distance.

"Have fun on your trip," Heath said with a smile.

"Thanks." She didn't look excited.

"What about the hives?" Heath wondered. "Did you find someone to check on them?"

"Yes," said Ali quickly. "Tam is going to watch out for them. I gave her a number to call if she sees anything of concern. There's another beekeeper on the south side of the county."

"Great." Heath didn't feel great. He wanted to offer to keep an eye out, which was bizarre given the circumstances. She didn't need him, obviously. She never had. And that's why he needed to go back to campus early.

"I hope it works out, then," he offered, suspecting she was anxious to part ways. "I hope your insurance comes through."

"It won't," she sighed. "I already checked into it."

"Are you serious?"

"Natural calamities aren't covered under what I signed up for." She motioned at her pretty top. "Thus the job interview."

"I'm sorry," said Heath.

"Me, too."

"It doesn't sound very fair." Heath didn't like the idea of Ali having to work another job just to be a beekeeper, but it wasn't his business.

She shrugged. "Life's not fair, Heath. I think we both know that, and I just don't have the time or energy to fight it anymore." She studied the tree house again, and he thought she looked impressed. "With a little good and a lot of God, I'll take care of it somehow."

"You always do." Heath shook his head at her tenacity. "I'm sure next year will be better."

"Right." Ali gave him a hopeful smile. "After a couple years, maybe we'll be thriving and I'll be able to quit the outside job."

"I wish you the best."

"You, too, Heath." Ali motioned toward the

tree house. "Thanks for fixing that up. I know it was inconvenient with all you had to do."

Heath nodded. "No problem. I promised him."

"Thank you for keeping your promises. I guess we'll see you later, then." Ali gave a little wave. "Have a good summer."

"You, too." There was so much distance between them it didn't make sense to close it, Heath decided. A handshake would be weird. A hug would be a little too friendly and torture for him. She had enough on her plate without worrying about his feelings. "Take care."

"Thanks."

Heath started back for the house, resisting the urge to see if Ali was still watching like he wanted to do. No, he wanted to do more than that, he thought suddenly. He wanted to pack his bags and go with them. He wanted to hold her hand, to put his arms around her, to listen to her laugh and to kiss her at sunset. He bit the inside of his lip, allowing himself to think about what that would be like, but the sweet yearning was followed by a chest pain that made him press his heart with his palm. He'd never dreaded a new semester before. Everything had changed.

The bench beneath Ali jolted her into the air, then bounced her from side to side like she was in a washing machine. She grabbed the sides of her seat and concentrated on her son's face. Charlie had one hand on the side of the boat with his face upturned to the sun, and his eyes were shut. Salty sea spray spritzed over the sides as they sped to the next fishing hole, bouncing over waves that felt like boulders, but Charlie only whooped and giggled. "He sounds like his dad," Ali started to say, but no one was listening. Even with another little boy and his father, and a crew onboard, she felt isolated, just as she had the first few months after she became a widow.

"Mom!" Ali looked, and Charlie pointed at a pod of dolphins chasing their wake. She felt a smile reach the apples of her cheeks as the blustery wind tangled her hair. They were beautiful and so was her child. Thankfully, there was a photographer on board to capture these moments. She hoped it'd all been worth it—the sunburn, the nausea, smelly bait and slimy fish. Even asking for a break on the monthly loan.

Charlie had loved every minute of it. Ali was sure the fishing trip would be something he would treasure forever. Maybe now he could let go of the pain of not having his father here until they met again.

Her throat tightened. She'd managed to cross that painful threshold, but it'd taken longer for her son. Another year in Lagrasse had helped. She thought of Heath, again, and wished she'd thanked him more fervently for all he'd done. Charlie slept better, laughed more and, since his first day fishing yesterday, glowed with the joy of childhood innocence she'd thought he'd lost forever.

So far, with the help of their guide, he'd managed to reel in six fish, and although he was disappointed it wasn't red snapper season, he was determined to catch something all by himself. The boy had dreams of marlin fishing all night long and shared every detail with her during breakfast, which happened to still be churning in her stomach.

Ali groaned and held her sides. Charlie staggered over and plopped down beside her, hair whipping across his forehead in the persistent wind. When he grinned, she noticed his new tooth was beginning to come in. "This is so fun."

"I'm glad you're having a good time," said Ali.

"I'm living my best life."

She laughed. He slanted his head at her from under his ball cap, enthusiasm whirling in his eyes. "I wish Mr. Heath was here. He'd catch lots of fish."

Ali playfully tugged Charlie's ball cap, surprised he hadn't mentioned his dad, but she knew he was in his heart, a heart that was healing. "Me, too, Charlie. He did say he fished at the lake from the bank sometimes."

"Yes, but this is better, and he likes to fly. This feels like flying when we go really fast."

"He might have gotten sick."

"He could have taken some medicine like you gave me."

"I'm glad it's working."

"Do you think he'll be gone when we get back?" asked Charlie.

"He has summer school, remember? He was leaving right after us."

The boy frowned. "How long until he comes home?"

"In August sometime." August sounded far-away to Ali.

Charlie grunted. "I'll have to go back to school by then."

"Yes, but you do have me for the summer," Ali reminded him. "Piper will be fun to play with, too."

"She's a girl." Charlie scowled. "I wish Dad was still here," he added, as if knowing what was on her mind. "And Heath, too."

"I'm sorry, honeybee." It was the truth.

Ali watched their fellow fishermen jump from their seats as a reel started spinning, and her heart pinged, wishing Heath was there. Maybe he would have come if she'd invited him, but he seemed relieved she'd resurrected the fence between them. The clear boundary would keep them friendly so nobody got hurt. Charlie would only see him occasionally at the tree house or at church when he was in town.

She watched her son chat excitedly with the captain, feeling useless and wishing she had more fishing experience, but this wasn't about her, she reminded herself. Her son loved the sea. He always had. He was as passionate about it as she was about the things she loved—him, her bees, Tam, country music, pizza and…

She sucked in a breath as her son cast his line. The captain put a hand on his shoulder, and she wished desperately again that it was Heath. It felt right to think so. Heath helping Charlie. Heath talking about his dog. Heath close beside her. Listening to her ramble. Holding her hand. He'd repaired the tree house with an active wasp nest nearby, showed up at her house while her hives were under attack, offered his comfort and his support…and after all he'd been through. The salt air made her eyes watery again, and Ali blinked as her heart filled with thick, warm emotion. This wasn't supposed to happen. Not yet. Not now. She had a child to raise and a business to save. She had no expectations that love would strike twice in a lifetime. How had she fallen for an accounting professor with a fear of bees?

She released another groan. It made no sense. Life always seemed to hit her at the worst time, and this was doubly bad, because the man who could never be more than her neighbor had no real attachment to Lagrasse. He was all about his numbers and his students, his status on campus and in academic circles, she told herself.

She bit back sour regret. Well, she'd just have to get over it. For Charlie's sake. She was good at that. It was going to be a long summer, but Heath wouldn't be around. There was no reason for him to ever know.

After his intern left for the afternoon, Heath clicked off the computer and pushed his doodle pad away. His mind was tired of calculating. Sometimes, he just thought too much, his mind constantly analyzing and deducing, trying to work out answers before he arrived at the problem. He leaned back in his chair, resisting the urge to slide out of his shoes. There was a booth for the accounting department set up at June's job fair in the quad this afternoon, and he'd promised to drop by. With a deep breath, he scooted out of his chair and locked the office door behind him, hoping Trooper would understand if he was a few minutes late. He strolled around the sidewalks checking out other booths for the incoming freshmen with mild interest.

A bright yellow canopy caught his attention. The word *Honey* was emblazoned across it, and he stopped, his mind seeing Ali and her jars of golden nectar. How he missed her. And Charlie. And the house. The pastures. The tree house. Pushing Charlie on the swing. He wondered how their summer was going. They'd be back from their trip by now, but Charlie hadn't called. Heath wondered if he'd forgotten about him.

He strolled to the tent, and a lanky young man with a short beard smiled with enthusiasm. "Hi," said his host. "Are you familiar with the Bee Lab?"

Heath scanned the table's offerings of pamphlets, honey sticks and T-shirts. "There's a bee lab on the campus?"

"Yes, we have honeybees and do research with observation hives."

"How did I not know this?" wondered Heath. "What kind of research?"

"We study native pollinators, for starters." The boy gave a spiel about clover and tulip poplars.

Heath interjected, "I think I have tulip poplar trees on my property." This led to a conversation about honey color and flavors, and before he knew it, Heath was reaching in his pocket to buy a jar of honey and a shirt. He hesitated when he was asked his size. "Youth small," he said.

"Do you have a son or daughter?" asked the student.

"Um...no." Heath's throat caught, and for

some reason, he felt like he was going to cry. He wanted a son. He wanted a family. Why couldn't he bring himself to make a real effort, try again, even if the family wasn't from scratch? What would he have to lose adopting a child into his life who was already in his heart? "I have a little friend," Heath explained. "I wish he was, but he's just a neighbor."

"A spoonful of honey beats a barrel of vinegar." The youth grinned.

Heath smiled. "I guess you're right." He couldn't imagine working on the house alone the past few months without Charlie around. Heath was handed his purchases.

"Thanks for supporting us."

"Thank you for doing your part," Heath replied. "Not everyone has the courage to work with bees, and we need them." He continued his job fair tour, noting clouds rolling in for an afternoon rain shower. He suddenly wished he'd put a canopy of some sort over the tree house after all. He'd have to do it when he got back.

Heath paused in front of the giant football stadium that held thousands of people. He'd only attended a few home games in his time here. It was quiet now. The students in his summer class were restless, bored and lacking the enthusiasm he saw at the beginning of the fall semester. A university was not meant to be a stopping place.

A settlement. A home. It was silly, he thought, to rent a town house when he had a house in Lagrasse, and live vicariously through the hundreds of young people that came through his classrooms every year instead of having his own adventures. Columns and figures did not nourish him in any way. Thinking of all the things honey provided for humanity, he doubted for the first time in his life that it was really numbers that made the world go round.

Heath stared across the campus. When had he stopped living in the moment? He sighed. Probably since he'd decided to become a professor and surround himself with books and figures that would not disappoint or hurt him. In math, everything added up, and he had control of that. In relationships, he had none. Losing his dad after his divorce had wounded him in worse ways than a hundred bees. He'd never let himself form any other relationships. Too risky. Mom's passing had made him determined to seal his heart up tight, for good. Until Charlie came along. And Ali. Heath thought of Monk and smiled. His old friend was right. He could run numbers and solve problems anywhere in the world, but he couldn't have the life he really wanted unless he went back home. The walls of the university were safe, but safe was not living, as a little boy had once taught him.

Chapter Fifteen

❧

Ali almost melted with relief when she pulled into the driveway. Her lower back ached, and her feet hurt. Charlie snapped off his seat belt. "I'm going to the tree house!" he announced.

"Be careful," Ali called as he darted off without shutting the door. She watched him let himself through the back gate and dash across the yard. Apparently, scout day camp this week did not have enough sunburn and bug bites for him. His energy levels since school let out were boundless. Even the fishing trip had not slowed him down. She exhaled as she got out of the car. She wished she could say the same. Her job was wearing her out. Dealing with customers all day wasn't too bad, but being on her feet and staring at spreadsheets when she wasn't filling in at a register or unloading plants for other people to take home was not how she wanted to spend her life. She missed being in her own yard, the hum of bees, the companionship of her child. Even her kitchen, where she brewed salves and the lip balm that Tam couldn't keep in stock.

Lip balm. Ali sighed. She'd promised Tam another batch by Friday. It also sold out at the farmers market every weekend, but that was a good thing. Plodding into the house, Ali changed her clothes and started to warm some wax. A glass of water with fresh-squeezed lime revived her, and she stood at the kitchen window and surveyed the yard. All looked calm in the apiary. She'd saved only two of the new hives, and the remaining colonies were not producing as quickly as she'd hoped. It was a setback, but the job at the nursery would compensate for it. She sighed. If only she'd known about the wasp nest. If only the insurance had covered it. If only...

She shook her head, pushing away feelings for Heath she knew she had to overcome, because they would never be returned, never lead anywhere. For a few seconds, she allowed herself to contemplate whether or not she would leave Lagrasse if it meant finding love again, but she quickly forced herself to concentrate on the concoction for her balms.

Weary, she turned everything off after one batch. The house was too quiet. Slipping on her cork bed sandals, she stretched her toes and plodded outside to the backyard. In just a few weeks, it'd be time to start collecting honey.

She tapped her thumbs and tried not to worry about her debts. She'd make it. She had Tam, her church family and God.

Ali walked over to make sure there was water in the birdbaths for the bees to use and saw someone had filled them up. She scrunched her forehead. Tam had come by to drop off a check but left it under the door. It must have been her. Ali wandered down to the ditch and searched for any sign of Charlie. She missed the sound of Trooper's commanding barks. With a faint smile of surrender, she realized her son needed a dog. It wasn't a substitute for their neighbor, or for a father, but it'd make her boy happy.

Contemplating the idea, she strolled into the woods. It'd rained the day before, and the undergrowth was still damp, the air earthy, the leaves on the trees shining and clean. The distant echo of her son's laughter pieced the air, and she followed the sound. Then she heard a bark and broke into a jog. Bursting into the clearing of the tree house, she stopped short in wonder. Charlie was in the giant beech, looking over the rail, and Trooper was trying to scramble up the small rope ladder Heath had hung for her son. The dog spotted her and yelped in delight. He bounced over, and Ali dropped to her knees. Trooper's paws hit her shoulders, and he nuzzled her neck with sloppy, wet kisses. Ali squeezed her eyes shut and laughed. "What are you doing here, you silly dog?" she cried.

Charlie shouted, "Trooper's here, Mom! Trooper's back!"

"I know, I see that," said Ali. She patted the dog until he calmed down and trotted back to the tree. She'd been right. Her son needed a dog. Maybe... Ali looked toward the Underwood home. Did this mean Heath was home? Surely he hadn't left his beloved collie behind with tenants.

"Hey, Ali."

The quiet voice made her spin around. He was three yards away with a small smile on his face. He wore khakis and a white shirt with the sleeves rolled up. The dark tortoiseshell glasses were in his chest pocket. He'd had a haircut and looked smart. Suave. Handsome. Ali's stomach cartwheeled, and she sucked in a breath but let it back out as a laugh to disguise her appraisal. "You're home." She couldn't keep the delight out of her voice. "But how?" She looked back at the silly, relentless dog then back at Heath. "Is everything okay?"

He put his hands in his pockets and crossed the distance between them. "Everything's fine."

"I thought you had class on campus."

He gave a half nod. "I did."

"It's over? Are you back for the roofers?"

He gave a shrug. "Yeah, but that's not for a few weeks."

"Oh." Ali didn't understand.

Heath stared at her for a long second, then seemed to collect himself. "I got a little homesick." He gave a sheepish chuckle. "That hasn't happened in a while. I used not to be able to wait to leave all Mom and Dad's clutter behind after seeing them."

"That's gone now."

"Yes, and I've cleaned everything out of the town house. Even my office."

"You did what?"

"I swapped my class with another professor who wanted to be on campus," said Heath. "I think working remotely suits me better for now." He cleared his throat and found something on the ground between them to study. "I also heard about a vacancy at Lagrasse Community College this fall."

"Here?" said Ali in surprise. "That would be amazing. You'd be home. I mean, you'd be… around."

"Just across the pasture." Heath smiled. "I hope you're okay with that. I know you were hoping for bee-loving tenants."

"Oh, no," stammered Ali, mind spinning.

"Hi, Mr. Heath!" shouted Charlie from the tree house.

"Hey, Charlie. How was the fishing trip?"

"It was awesome, but I didn't catch any snapper."

"You didn't call."

"Mom made me write you a letter. She said you were busy."

"Did you mail it?"

"I don't know," the boy hollered.

Heath gave Ali a questioning look as Charlie scrambled down the tree. She flushed. "I gave him a stamp. It may have not made it to the mailbox."

"Charlie doesn't bother me. You don't, either. Ever." Heath stopped, and his face turned pink.

Ali felt a spark of hope. "Are you sure? Between my bees and fences and little boys, I'm not always sure where we stand. And I know most of that is my fault."

He moved closer, making her heart skip a beat. "Believe it or not, I happen to be developing a taste for honey."

"Is that so?" Ali felt her lips pull into a grin despite the fact he was studying her face like it was a puzzle he wanted to put together.

"Yes. A wise beekeeper once told me the sweet life is worth a little sting or two."

She laughed and was flooded with happiness. "Charlie will be beside himself."

Heath looked sideways, and she followed his

gaze. Charlie was watching them from where he'd climbed down from the tree. He broke into a smile and opened his mouth to speak, but Trooper interrupted him first. The dog nipped at his shorts and playfully dashed a few steps away, and the boy gave chase. Ali laughed nervously.

"Will you...be beside yourself?" Heath's tone was low, hesitant but sincere.

Ali searched his blue-eyed gaze. "I am," she admitted. She swallowed nervously. "In fact, I've even had the nerve to wonder what life in Alabama might be like."

"It's okay," he said with a small smile. "It'd be better with family."

She nodded in understanding. "Lagrasse is family, isn't it?"

Heath reached for her hand. She met him halfway and clutched his fingers. "It is," he murmured. "I've come to realize it could offer more than I ever dreamed. That's why I came back."

Ali flooded with emotions she was helpless to resist. She loved him, but was her life too much? "It's more than I deserve or ever hoped for, despite the wasps and the loan and—"

Heath stole her breath by touching her cheek with his warm hand. He smelled like soap and ink. "And me?" he whispered.

"No, you're safe," she said, knowing it was true.

"You'd be safe with me," he promised. "If you

wanted to try, because I... I'll never be happy anywhere without you and Charlie around." His cheeks reddened, and Ali wanted to kiss each one. She gave him a small, inviting smile to continue. "Because I love you," Heath admitted. "I'm here. Willing to get stung if it means a chance with you, and if you think you're ready. I can wait if you're not. I'll learn to live without it if it can't be. For Charlie's sake."

Tears pricked Ali's eyes. "I am ready," she said. "All this time I thought my only purpose was to raise my son and survive, but I know God sent me here for more than that. Something better. He knew what I needed better than I did."

"A second chance?"

"A second love," choked Ali. "Heath, I would never hurt you any more than I would my own child."

"You are a queen, Ali Harding," Heath whispered. He brushed a lock of hair from her forehead and touched her nose with his. Her knees melted like her beeswax. She held his gaze until he dropped his lips onto hers, and her eyes fluttered shut. A happy, buzzing sensation enveloped her as a pleasant shudder rippled down her spine. Ali was safe. Heath was at peace. And there was a sparkling, electric love between them and her little boy. She wrapped her arms around him and let him into her heart.

Epilogue

Heath Underwood stood outside the doors to the old country church. Scarlet trees and silver tombstones marked the passage of time beneath the autumn sun behind it. The tall spire glowed a heavenly shade of white. Heath's heart trembled, but he clung to the happiness and hope he already knew.

Mounting the steps to the freshly painted doors, he pushed them open with a gulp of courage and strode through the lobby to the sanctuary, pausing to examine a room filled with family and friends. He resisted the urge to count heads and multiply them by the number of pews, instead focusing on the rainbow streaming through the stained glass windows. His brother and Monk waited at the pulpit with teasing grins. Heath marched the distance to meet them, accepting their firm handshakes while trying to disguise the thundering butterflies in his stomach. He smoothed down his dark blue waistcoat and straightened his small yellow boutonniere.

Sister Lovell struck the first chords on the bellowing old organ, and the pews creaked behind him as the congregation rose to their feet. Heath took a deep breath and dared to look over his shoulder. He joined everyone else in gasping at the first sight of Ali. She moved calmly and deliberately, but not without the usual merry glint in her eye. She was a vision in vanilla silk. The slim-fitting gown was overlaid with a wispy layer of tulle and belted high on her waist with a wide ribbon. Heath's new father-in-law, who enjoyed quoting baseball statistics and sharing the antics of his grandson, escorted her by the arm. He gave Heath a comforting smile that warmed his heart but tightened his throat. Charlie led the entire procession, unceremoniously tugging the flower girl and ring bearer along. His eyes brightened when he met Heath's gaze, and they grinned at one another.

When a smiling, modest Ali was presented to him, Heath reached for the warmth and security of her hand, knowing he would treasure her touch forever and hold sacred the vows he would make with her and his new son today. Tears he'd buried deeply after the losses he'd endured were set free when Ali turned to him and whispered *yes*. It all ended with a kiss that made Charlie giggle quietly, then Heath felt himself floating back down the aisle and through the doors to the front lawn.

Fluttering white canopies made the churchyard look like a carnival. Ali turned to him with tearstained cheeks when he squeezed her hand at the entrance to the covered tables and desserts. "Have I said lately how much I love you?" she murmured.

"You have, but I don't know why."

Her eyes widened in surprise. "You are the kindest, most patient man I have ever met, and besides being handsome and smart, you've given me a second chance to have a family and be loved."

Heath put an arm around her waist and pulled her to him. "I have loved you since the first moment you scolded me for taking down your fence."

She chuckled. "You mean *your* fence."

"You are the most fearless and determined person I've ever met," Heath confessed. "You have faith I can only aspire to, but I'm working on it."

"You have more than you know," Ali promised. "Just look at who you've just taken on. You're brave."

"You make me brave and remind me who I can be," Heath insisted. "It's an honor." Her eyes teared, and Heath leaned down and dropped another kiss on her satin lips. "And Charlie is the cherry on top."

Ali smiled and pointed at the spread of refreshments that surrounded a giant tower of chocolatey-brown cupcakes catered by her favorite bakery. Little honeybees made of spun sugar decorated each one. "Are you sure you don't mean the frosting on top?"

Heath laughed, but Ali grew serious as voices burst out of the church doors behind them. "I always believed God gave second chances, but I never let myself believe those blessings were meant for me," she whispered. "What have I done to deserve happiness twice in a lifetime?"

Heath gave her a tight embrace. "Lived for others and believed?" he whispered. "Happiness isn't a onetime gift, Ali. We just have to look for it when we lose it instead of trying to go it alone."

"I'm glad I get to be happy again with you," she murmured.

Before Heath could reply, Charlie raced by, all pomp and circumstance forgotten at the sight of so many goodies. "Maybe we both had to learn how precious and fleeting love can be," said Ali.

"And believe that lightning can strike twice," Heath added. Charlie whooped from a few feet away, and he chuckled. "Or three times."

"Well, I hope there's a fourth," Ali admitted.

"I can't wait to grow our little hive and add a few more bumbles to our family."

Heath squeezed her hand in a firm grip of devotion and led her to their table and the rest of their lives.

* * * * *

Dear Reader,

I hope you enjoyed meeting the characters in the new setting of Lagrasse, Georgia, who embraced the beauty (and challenges) of the simple life with family and friends. This tiny town reminds me of one of my favorite places south of my home, where West Point Lake straddles the Alabama-Georgia line. It's a beautiful area with state parks and small towns where I like to hike and kayak. There's also a growing movement in this neck of the woods to produce honey, which we depend on as a sweetener in our house, and writing about it gave me an opportunity to share the importance of these insects in our lives. I hope it was as interesting and educational for you as it was for me, although I barely scratched the surface. Most importantly, I hope I captured the essence of how important family is to all of us and that we must remember that those who go before us would want us to continue finding happiness and developing relationships. Family is love—from either side of the veil.

Thank you to my editors and interns who work so diligently in the background with me on my books. Shout out to Julie Hammond for her creative suggestion for the name of the bakery. Watch for the Last Re-Torte Bakery in the next story set in Lagrasse, and thank you for reading my books, sharing them with friends and posting reviews online. Your support makes my dream job possible. I wish you joy.

Warmly,
Danielle Thorne